"Terrifying, hopeful, and all too relevant."   —*People*

"In spare, crystalline prose, Hamid conveys the experience of living in a city under siege with sharp, stabbing immediacy. He shows just how swiftly ordinary life—with all its banal rituals and routines—can morph into the defensive crouch of life in a war zone . . . [and] how insidiously violence alters the calculus of daily life. . . . By mixing the real and the surreal, and using old fairy-tale magic, Hamid has created a fictional universe that captures the global perils percolating beneath today's headlines."   —Michiko Kakutani, *The New York Times*

"Lyrical and urgent . . . [Hamid] peels away the dross of bigotry to expose the beauty of our common humanity."   —*O, The Oprah Magazine*

"Hamid rewrites the world as a place thoroughly, gorgeously, and permanently overrun by refugees and migrants. . . . The novel feels immediately canonical, so firm and unerring is Hamid's understanding of our time and its most pressing questions."   —NewYorker.com

"Taut but haunting."   —*Vanity Fair*

"In gossamer-fine sentences, *Exit West* weaves a pulse-raising tale of menace and romance, a parable of our refugee crisis, and a poignant vignette of love won and lost. . . . Let the word go forth: Hamid has written his most lyrical and piercing novel yet, destined to be one of this year's landmark achievements."   —Minneapolis *Star Tribune*

"Spellbinding."   —BuzzFeed

PRAISE FOR *EXIT WEST*

"It was as if Hamid knew what was going to happen to America and the world, and gave us a road map to our future.... At once terrifying and ... oddly hopeful."   —Ayelet Waldman, *The New York Times Book Review*

"Moving, audacious, and indelibly human."

—*Entertainment Weekly* ("A" rating)

"This is the best writing of Hamid's career.... Readers will find themselves going back and savoring each paragraph several times before moving on. He's that good."   —NPR.org

"Hamid exploits fiction's capacity to elicit empathy and identification to imagine a better world. It is also a possible world. *Exit West* does not lead to utopia, but to a near future and the dim shapes of strangers that we can see through a distant doorway. All we have to do is step through it and meet them."   —Viet Thanh Nguyen, *The New York Times Book Review*

"Good novels expose and interpret the particular condition of the humans in their charge, and this is what Hamid has achieved here. If in its physical and perilous immediacy Nadia and Saeed's condition is alien to the mass of us, *Exit West* makes a final, certain declaration of affinity: 'We are all migrants through time.'" —*The Washington Post*

"Powerfully evokes the violence and anxiety of lives lived 'under the drone-crossed sky.'" —*Time*

"If we are looking for the story of our time, one that can project a future that is both more bleak and more hopeful than that which we can yet envision, this novel is faultless." —*The Boston Globe*

"A little like the eerily significant Margaret Atwood novel, this love story amid the rubble of violence, uncertainty, and modernity feels at once otherworldly and all too real." —*New York* magazine

"Hamid has said that 'part of the great political crisis we face in the world today is a failure to imagine plausible desirable futures,' and that 'fiction can imagine differently.' *Exit West* does so, and beautifully. May Hamid's hopes turn out to be as prescient as his concerns already are." —*San Francisco Chronicle*

"Brilliant . . . [Hamid] highlights the stark reality of the refugee experience and the universal struggle of dislocation." —*Newsday*

"[A] meticulously crafted, ambitious story of many layers, many geopolitical realities, many lives and circumstances . . . Here is the world, he seems to be saying, the direction we're hurtling in. How are we going to mitigate the damage we've done?"

—*The New York Review of Books*

"What is remarkable about Hamid's narrative is that war is not, in fact, able to marginalize the 'precious mundanity' of everyday life. Instead—and herein lies Hamid's genius as a storyteller—the mundanity, the minor joys of life, like bringing flowers to a lover, smoking a joint, and looking at stars, compete with the horrors of war."

—*Los Angeles Times*

"Hamid's writing . . . makes *Exit West* an absorbing read, but the ideas he expresses and the future he's bold enough to imagine define it as an unmissable one." —*The Atlantic*

"Brilliant." —*Vulture*

"[An] ambitious and far-roaming tale of migration and adventure . . . which feels like something quite new." —*The New Republic*

"A dark fable for our turbulent time, *Exit West* . . . portrays a world of transience, violence, and insecurity that rhymes with our world of porous borders and rabid tribalists." —*The Dallas Morning News*

"Spare and haunting, it's magical realism meets the all-too-real."

—*W* magazine

"With great empathy, Hamid skillfully chronicles the manic condition of involuntary migration. . . . *Exit West* rattles our perception of home."

—*St. Louis Post-Dispatch*

"Reading Mohsin Hamid's penetrating, prescient new novel feels like bearing witness to events that are unfolding before us in real time."

—*The Seattle Times*

"If there is one book everyone should read ASAP, it is Mohsin Hamid's *Exit West*. . . . Short, unsentimental, deeply intimate, and so very powerful."

—*Goop*

"A sly and intelligent book, written with Hamid's extraordinary eye for character—their desires, hopes, grudges, and disappointments—all those 'faulty human things' that keep us alive and make us real. But what truly sets the book apart, both in Hamid's oeuvre and contemporary fiction, is its warmth and generosity to its readers—something we need more of from books in our morally exhausting times."

—*Guernica*

"Urgent and much needed . . . An antidote of sorts (one can only hope) in this moment of xenophobic fear and mistrust."

—*Mother Jones*

"Brilliant . . . If you're numb to the unending talk relating to migration policy, the platitudes and the protest slogans, this book provides a way to reignite much-needed empathy because, above all, Hamid reminds us that no matter hard governments try, they can never really close doors."

—*Toronto Star*

"A beautiful rendering of the lives hidden in the folds of war."

—*The A. V. Club*

"While we've permitted ourselves to go soft, we can be thankful for the writers in the rest of the world who continue to write in the tradition of our greatest literary works. No surprise, then, that Mohsin Hamid belongs in that pattern. . . . A writer celebrating the possibility of hope. That's what makes his latest novel so profound."

—*CounterPunch*

EXIT WEST

EXIT WEST

A NOVEL

MOHSIN HAMID

RIVERHEAD BOOKS

New York

RIVERHEAD BOOKS
An imprint of Penguin Random House LLC
375 Hudson Street
New York, New York 10014

The Library of Congress has catalogued the
Riverhead hardcover edition as follows:

Names: Hamid, Mohsin, author.
Title: Exit west : a novel / Mohsin Hamid.
Description: New York : Riverhead Books, 2017.
Identifiers: LCCN 2016036296 | ISBN 9780735212176
(hardcover)
Subjects: LCSH: Refugees—Fiction. | BISAC:
FICTION / Political. | FICTION / Cultural Heritage.
| FICTION / Literary. | GSAFD: Love stories.
Classification: LCC PS3558.A42169 E95 2017 | DDC
813/.54—dc23
LC record available at https://lccn.loc.gov/2016036296
p.   cm.

First Riverhead hardcover edition: March 2017
First Riverhead trade paperback edition: March 2018
Riverhead trade paperback ISBN: 9780735212206

Riverhead international trade paperback
ISBN: 9780525535065

Printed in the United States of America
16th Printing

Book design by Marysarah Quinn

FOR NAVED AND NASIM

ONE

N A CITY SWOLLEN BY REFUGEES but still mostly at peace, or at least not yet openly at war, a young man met a young woman in a classroom and did not speak to her. For many days. His name was Saeed and her name was Nadia and he had a beard, not a full beard, more a studiously maintained stubble, and she was always clad from the tips of her toes to the bottom of her jugular notch in a flowing black robe. Back then people continued to enjoy the luxury of wearing more or less what they wanted to wear, clothing and hair wise, within certain bounds of course, and so these choices meant something.

It might seem odd that in cities teetering at the edge of the abyss young people still go to class—in this case an evening class on corporate identity and product branding—but that is

3

the way of things, with cities as with life, for one moment we are pottering about our errands as usual and the next we are dying, and our eternally impending ending does not put a stop to our transient beginnings and middles until the instant when it does.

Saeed noticed that Nadia had a beauty mark on her neck, a tawny oval that sometimes, rarely but not never, moved with her pulse.

NOT LONG AFTER NOTICING THIS, Saeed spoke to Nadia for the first time. Their city had yet to experience any major fighting, just some shootings and the odd car bombing, felt in one's chest cavity as a subsonic vibration like those emitted by large loudspeakers at music concerts, and Saeed and Nadia had packed up their books and were leaving class.

In the stairwell he turned to her and said, "Listen, would you like to have a coffee," and after a brief pause added, to make it seem less forward, given her conservative attire, "in the cafeteria?"

Nadia looked him in the eye. "You don't say your evening prayers?" she asked.

Saeed conjured up his most endearing grin. "Not always. Sadly."

Her expression did not change.

So he persevered, clinging to his grin with the mounting desperation of a doomed rock climber: "I think it's personal. Each of us has his own way. Or . . . her own way. Nobody's perfect. And, in any case—"

She interrupted him. "I don't pray," she said.

She continued to gaze at him steadily.

Then she said, "Maybe another time."

He watched as she walked out to the student parking area and there, instead of covering her head with a black cloth, as he expected, she donned a black motorcycle helmet that had been locked to a scuffed-up hundred-ish cc trail bike, snapped down her visor, straddled her ride, and rode off, disappearing with a controlled rumble into the gathering dusk.

THE NEXT DAY, at work, Saeed found himself unable to stop thinking of Nadia. Saeed's employer was an agency that specialized in the placement of outdoor advertising. They owned billboards all around the city, rented others, and struck deals for further space with the likes of bus lines, sports stadiums, and proprietors of tall buildings.

The agency occupied both floors of a converted townhouse and had over a dozen employees. Saeed was among the most junior, but his boss liked him and had tasked him with turning around a pitch to a local soap company that had to go out by email before five. Normally Saeed tried to do copious amounts of online research and customize his presentations as much as possible. "It's not a story if it doesn't have an audience," his boss was fond of saying, and for Saeed this meant trying to show a client that his firm truly understood their business, could really get under their skin and see things from their point of view.

But today, even though the pitch was important—every pitch was important: the economy was sluggish from mounting unrest and one of the first costs clients seemed to want to cut was outdoor advertising—Saeed couldn't focus. A large tree, overgrown and untrimmed, reared up from the tiny back lawn of his firm's townhouse, blocking out the sunlight in such a manner that the back lawn had been reduced mostly to dirt and a few wisps of grass, interspersed with a morning's worth of cigarette butts, for his boss had banned people from smoking indoors, and atop this tree Saeed had spotted a hawk constructing its nest. It worked tirelessly. Sometimes it floated at eye level, almost stationary in the wind, and then, with the tiniest movement of a wing, or even of the upturned feathers at one wingtip, it veered.

Saeed thought of Nadia and watched the hawk.

When he was at last running out of time he scrambled to prepare the pitch, copying and pasting from others he had done before. Only a smattering of the images he selected had anything particularly to do with soap. He took a draft to his boss and suppressed a wince while sliding it over.

But his boss seemed preoccupied and didn't notice. He just jotted some minor edits on the printout, handed it back to Saeed with a wistful smile, and said, "Send it out."

Something about his expression made Saeed feel sorry for him. He wished he had done a better job.

As SAEED'S EMAIL was being downloaded from a server and read by his client, far away in Australia a pale-skinned woman was sleeping alone in the Sydney neighborhood of Surry Hills. Her husband was in Perth on business. The woman wore only a long T-shirt, one of his, and a wedding ring. Her torso and left leg were covered by a sheet even paler than she was; her right leg and right hip were bare. On her right ankle, perched in the dip of her Achilles tendon, was the blue tattoo of a small mythological bird.

Her home was alarmed, but the alarm was not active. It had been installed by previous occupants, by others who had once called this place home, before the phenomenon referred to as the gentrification of this neighborhood had run as far as it had now run. The sleeping woman used the alarm only sporadically, mostly when her husband was absent, but on this night she had forgotten. Her bedroom window, four meters above the ground, was open, just a slit.

In the drawer of her bedside table were a half-full packet of birth control pills, last consumed three months ago, when she and her husband were still trying not to conceive, passports, checkbooks, receipts, coins, keys, a pair of handcuffs, and a few paper-wrapped sticks of unchewed chewing gum.

The door to her closet was open. Her room was bathed in the glow of her computer charger and wireless router, but the closet doorway was dark, darker than night, a rectangle of complete darkness—the heart of darkness. And out of this darkness, a man was emerging.

He too was dark, with dark skin and dark, woolly hair. He wriggled with great effort, his hands gripping either side of the doorway as though pulling himself up against gravity, or against the rush of a monstrous tide. His neck followed his head, tendons straining, and then his chest, his half-unbuttoned, sweaty, gray-and-brown shirt. Suddenly he paused in his exertions. He looked around the room. He looked at the sleeping woman, the shut bedroom door, the open window. He rallied himself again, fighting mightily to come in, but in desperate silence, the silence of a man struggling in an alley, on the ground, late at night, to free himself of hands clenched around his throat. But there were no hands around this man's throat. He wished only not to be heard.

With a final push he was through, trembling and sliding to the floor like a newborn foal. He lay still, spent. Tried not to pant. He rose.

His eyes rolled terribly. Yes: terribly. Or perhaps not so terribly. Perhaps they merely glanced about him, at the woman, at the bed, at the room. Growing up in the not infrequently perilous circumstances in which he had grown up, he was aware of the fragility of his body. He knew how little it took to make a man into meat: the wrong blow, the wrong gunshot, the wrong flick of a blade, turn of a car, presence of a microorganism in a handshake, a cough. He was aware that alone a person is almost nothing.

The woman who slept, slept alone. He who stood above her, stood alone. The bedroom door was shut. The window was open. He chose the window. He was through it in an instant, dropping silkily to the street below.

WHILE THIS INCIDENT was occurring in Australia, Saeed was picking up fresh bread for dinner and heading home. He was an independent-minded, grown man, unmarried, with a decent post and a good education, and as was the case in those days in his city with most independent-minded, grown men, unmarried, with decent posts and good educations, he lived with his parents.

Saeed's mother had the commanding air of a schoolteacher, which she formerly was, and his father the slightly lost bearing of a university professor, which he continued to be—though on reduced wages, for he was past the official retirement age and had been forced to seek out visiting faculty work. Both of Saeed's parents, the better part of a lifetime ago, had chosen respectable professions in a country that would wind up doing rather badly by its respectable professionals. Security and status were to be found only in other, quite different pursuits. Saeed had been born to them late, so late that his mother had believed her doctor was being cheeky when he asked if she thought she was pregnant.

Their small flat was in a once handsome building, with an ornate though now crumbling facade that dated back to the colonial era, in a once upscale, presently crowded and commercial, part of town. It had been partitioned from a much larger flat and comprised three rooms: two modest bedrooms and a third chamber they used for sitting, dining, entertaining, and watching television. This third chamber was also modest in size but had tall windows and a usable, if narrow, balcony, with a view down an alley and straight up a boulevard to a dry fountain that once gushed and sparkled in the sunlight. It was the sort of view that might command a slight premium during gentler, more prosperous times, but would be most undesirable in times of conflict, when it would be squarely in the path of heavy machine-gun and rocket fire as fighters advanced into this part of town: a view like staring down the barrel of a rifle. Location, location, location, the realtors say. Geography is destiny, respond the historians.

War would soon erode the facade of their building as though it had accelerated time itself, a day's toll outpacing that of a decade.

WHEN SAEED'S PARENTS FIRST MET they were the same age as were Saeed and Nadia when they first did. The elder pair's was a love marriage, a marriage between strangers not arranged by their families, which, in their circles, while not unprecedented, was still less than common.

They met at the cinema, during the intermission of a film about a resourceful princess. Saeed's mother spied his father having a cigarette and was struck by his similarity to the male lead in the movie. This similarity was not entirely accidental:

though a little shy and very bookish, Saeed's father styled himself after the popular film stars and musicians of his day, as did most of his friends. But Saeed's father's myopia combined with his personality to give him an expression that was genuinely dreamy, and this, understandably, resulted in Saeed's mother thinking he not merely looked the part, but embodied it. She decided to make her approach.

Standing in front of Saeed's father she proceeded to talk animatedly with a friend while ignoring the object of her desire. He noticed her. He listened to her. He summoned the nerve to speak to her. And that, as they were both fond of saying when recounting the story of their meeting in subsequent years, was that.

Saeed's mother and father were both readers, and, in different ways, debaters, and they were frequently to be seen in the early days of their romance meeting surreptitiously in bookshops. Later, after their marriage, they would while away afternoons reading together in cafés and restaurants, or, when the weather was suitable, on their balcony. He smoked and she said she didn't, but often, when the ash of his seemingly forgotten cigarette grew impossibly extended, she took it from his fingers, trimmed it softly against an ashtray, and pulled a long and rather rakish drag before returning it, daintily.

The cinema where Saeed's parents met was long gone by the

time their son met Nadia, as were the bookshops they favored and most of their beloved restaurants and cafés. It was not that cinemas and bookshops, restaurants and cafés had vanished from the city, just that many of those that had been there before were there no longer. The cinema they remembered so fondly had been replaced by a shopping arcade for computers and electronic peripherals. This building had taken the same name as the cinema that preceded it: both once had the same owner, and the cinema had been so famous as to have become a byword for that locality. When walking by the arcade, and seeing that old name on its new neon sign, sometimes Saeed's father, sometimes Saeed's mother, would remember, and smile. Or remember, and pause.

SAEED'S PARENTS did not have sex until their wedding night. Of the two, Saeed's mother found it more uncomfortable, but she was also the more keen, and so she insisted on repeating the act twice more before dawn. For many years, their balance remained thus. Generally speaking, she was voracious in bed. Generally speaking, he was obliging. Perhaps because she did not, until Saeed's conception two decades later, get pregnant, and assumed therefore she could not, she was able to have sex with abandon, without, that is, thought of consequences or the distractions of child-rearing. Meanwhile his typical manner, throughout the first half of their marriage, at her strenuous advances, was that of a man pleasantly surprised. She found mustaches and being taken from behind erotic. He found her carnal and motivating.

After Saeed was born, the frequency with which his parents had sex dipped notably, and it continued to decline going forward. A uterus began to prolapse, an erection became harder to maintain. During this phase, Saeed's father started to be cast, or to cast himself, more and more often, as the one who tried to initiate sex. Saeed's mother would sometimes wonder whether he did this out of genuine desire or habit or simply for closeness. She tried her best to respond. He would eventually come to be rebuffed by his own body at least as much as by hers.

In the last year of the life they shared together, the year that was already well under way when Saeed met Nadia, they had sex only thrice. As many times in a year as on their wedding night. But his father always kept a mustache, at his mother's insistence. And they never once changed their bed: its headboard like the posts of a banister, almost demanding to be gripped.

IN WHAT SAEED'S FAMILY called their living room there was a telescope, black and sleek. It had been given to Saeed's father by his father, and Saeed's father had given it in turn to Saeed, but since Saeed still lived at home, this meant the telescope continued to sit where it always sat, on its tripod in a corner, underneath an intricate clipper ship that sailed inside a glass bottle on the sea of a triangular shelf.

The sky above their city had become too polluted for much in the way of stargazing. But on cloudless nights after a daytime rain, Saeed's father would sometimes bring out the telescope, and the family would sip green tea on their balcony, enjoying a breeze, and take turns to look up at objects whose light, often, had been emitted before any of these three viewers had been born—light from other centuries, only now reaching Earth. Saeed's father called this time-travel.

On one particular night, though, in fact the night after he had struggled to prepare his firm's pitch to the soap company, Saeed was absentmindedly scanning along a trajectory that ran below the horizon. In his eyepiece were windows and walls and rooftops, sometimes stationary, sometimes whizzing by at incredible speed.

"I think he's looking at young ladies," Saeed's father said to his mother.

"Behave yourself, Saeed," said his mother.

"Well, he is your son."

"I never needed a telescope."

"Yes, you preferred to operate short-range."

Saeed shook his head and tacked upward.

"I see Mars," he said. And indeed he did. The second-nearest planet, its features indistinct, the color of a sunset after a dust storm.

Saeed straightened and held up his phone, directing its camera at the heavens, consulting an application that indicated the names of celestial bodies he did not know. The Mars it showed was more detailed as well, though it was of course a Mars from another moment, a bygone Mars, fixed in memory by the application's creator.

In the distance Saeed's family heard the sound of automatic gunfire, flat cracks that were not loud and yet carried to them cleanly. They sat a little longer. Then Saeed's mother suggested they return inside.

WHEN SAEED AND NADIA finally had coffee together in the cafeteria, which happened the following week, after the very next session of their class, Saeed asked her about her conservative and virtually all-concealing black robe.

"If you don't pray," he said, lowering his voice, "why do you wear it?"

They were sitting at a table for two by a window, overlooking snarled traffic on the street below. Their phones rested screens-down between them, like the weapons of desperadoes at a parley.

She smiled. Took a sip. And spoke, the lower half of her face obscured by her cup.

"So men don't fuck with me," she said.

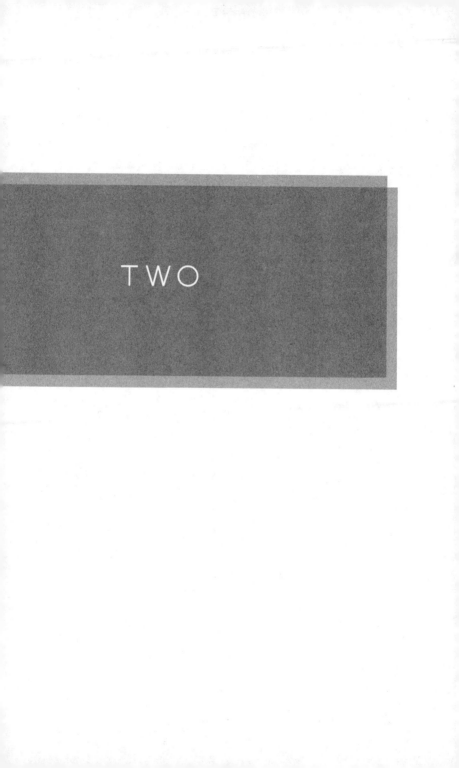

TWO

W HEN NADIA WAS A CHILD, her favorite subject was art, even though art was taught only once a week and she did not consider herself particularly talented as an artist. She had gone to a school that emphasized rote memorization, for which she was by temperament particularly ill-suited, and so she spent a great deal of time doodling in the margins of her textbooks and notebooks, hunched over to hide curlicues and miniature woodland universes from the eyes of her teachers. If they caught her, she would get a scolding, or occasionally a slap on the back of the head.

The art in Nadia's childhood home consisted of religious verses and photos of holy sites, framed and mounted on walls. Nadia's mother and sister were quiet women and her father a man who tried to be quiet, thinking this a virtue, but who none-theless came to a boil easily and often where Nadia was concerned. Her constant questioning and growing irreverence in matters of faith upset and frightened him. There was no physical violence in Nadia's home, and much giving to charity, but when after finishing university Nadia announced, to her family's utter horror, and to her own surprise for she had not planned to say it, that she was moving out on her own, an unmarried woman, the break involved hard words on all sides, from her father, from her mother, even more so from her sister, and perhaps most of all from Nadia herself, such that Nadia and her family both considered her thereafter to be without a family, something all of them, all four, for the rest of their lives, regretted, but which none of them would ever act to repair, partly out of stubbornness, partly out of bafflement at how to go about doing so, and partly because the impending descent of their city into the abyss would come before they realized that they had lost the chance.

Nadia's experiences during her first months as a single woman living on her own did, in some moments, equal or even surpass the loathsomeness and dangerousness that her family had warned her about. But she had a job at an insurance company, and she was determined to survive, and so she did. She secured a room of her own atop the house of a widow, a record player and small collection of vinyl, a circle of acquaintances among the city's free spirits, and a connection to a discreet and nonjudgmental female gynecologist. She learned how to dress for self-protection, how best to deal with aggressive men and with the police, and with aggressive men who were the police, and always to trust her instincts about situations to avoid or to exit immediately.

But sitting at her desk at the insurance company, on an afternoon of handling executive auto policy renewals by phone, when she received an instant message from Saeed asking if she would like to meet, her work posture was still hunched over, as it had been when she was a schoolgirl, and she was still doodling, as always, in the margins of the printouts before her.

THEY MET at a Chinese restaurant of Nadia's choosing, this not being a class night. The family that used to run the place, after arriving in the city following the Second World War, and flourishing there for three generations, had recently sold up and emigrated to Canada. But prices remained reasonable, and the standard of food had not yet fallen. The dining area had a darkened, opium-den ambience, in contrast to other Chinese restaurants in the city. It was distinctively lit by what looked like candle-filled paper lanterns, but were in fact plastic, illuminated by flame-shaped, electronically flickering bulbs.

Nadia arrived first and watched Saeed enter and walk to her table. He had, as he often did, an amused expression in his bright eyes, not mocking, but as though he saw the humor in things, and this in turn amused her and made her warm to him. She resisted smiling, knowing it would not be long for him to smile, and indeed he smiled before reaching the table, and his smile was then returned.

"I like it," he said, indicating their surroundings. "Sort of mysterious. Like we could be anywhere. Well, not anywhere, but not here."

"Have you ever traveled abroad?"

He shook his head. "I want to."

"Me too."

"Where would you go?"

She considered him for a while. "Cuba."

"Cuba! Why?"

"I don't know. It makes me think of music and beautiful old buildings and the sea."

"Sounds perfect."

"And you? Where would you pick? One place."

"Chile."

"So we both want to go to Latin America."

He grinned. "The Atacama Desert. The air is so dry, so clear, and there's so few people, almost no lights. And you can lie on your back and look up and see the Milky Way. All the stars like a splash of milk in the sky. And you see them slowly move. Because the Earth is moving. And you feel like you're lying on a giant spinning ball in space."

Nadia watched Saeed's features. In that moment they were tinged with wonder, and he looked, despite his stubble, boylike. He struck her as a strange sort of man. A strange and attractive sort of man.

Their waiter came to take their order. Neither Nadia nor Saeed chose a soft drink, preferring tea and water, and when their food arrived neither used chopsticks, both being, at least while under observation, more confident of their skills with a fork instead. Despite initial instances of awkwardness, or rather of disguised shyness, they found it mostly easy to talk to one another, which always comes as something of a relief on a first proper date. They spoke quietly, cautious not to attract the attention of nearby diners. Their meal was finished too soon.

They next faced the problem that confronted all young people in the city who wanted to continue in one another's company past a certain hour. During the day there were parks, and campuses, and restaurants, cafés. But at night, after dinner, unless one had access to a home where such things were safe and permitted, or had a car, there were few places to be alone. Saeed's family had a car, but it was being repaired, and so he had come by scooter. And Nadia had a home, but it was tricky, in more ways than one, to have a man over.

Still, she decided to invite him.

Saeed seemed surprised and extremely excited when she suggested he come.

"Nothing is going to happen," she explained. "I want to make that clear. When I say you should come over, I'm not saying I want your hands on me."

"No. Of course."

Saeed's expression had grown traumatized.

But Nadia nodded. And while her eyes were warm, she did not smile.

REFUGEES HAD OCCUPIED many of the open places in the city, pitching tents in the greenbelts between roads, erecting lean-tos next to the boundary walls of houses, sleeping rough on sidewalks and in the margins of streets. Some seemed to be trying to re-create the rhythms of a normal life, as though it were completely natural to be residing, a family of four, under a sheet of plastic propped up with branches and a few chipped bricks. Others stared out at the city with what looked like anger, or surprise, or supplication, or envy. Others didn't move at all: stunned, maybe, or resting. Possibly dying. Saeed and Nadia had to be careful when making turns not to run over an outstretched arm or leg.

As she nosed her motorcycle home, followed by Saeed on his scooter, Nadia did have several moments of questioning whether she had done the right thing. But she didn't change her mind.

There were two checkpoints on their way, one manned by police and another, newer one, manned by soldiers. The police didn't bother with them. The soldiers stopped everyone. They made Nadia remove her helmet, perhaps thinking she might be a man disguised as a woman, but when they saw this was not the case, they waved her through.

Nadia rented the top portion of a narrow building belonging to a widow whose children and grandchildren all lived abroad. This building had once been a single house, but it was constructed adjacent to a market that had subsequently grown past and around it. The widow had kept the middle floor for herself, converted the bottom floor into a shop that she let out to a seller of car-battery-based residential-power-backup systems, and given the uppermost floor to Nadia, who had overcome the widow's initial suspicions by claiming that she too was a widow, her husband a young infantry officer killed in battle, which, admittedly, was less than entirely true.

Nadia's flat comprised a studio room with an alcove kitchenette and a bathroom so small that showering without drenching the commode was impossible. But it opened onto a roof terrace that looked out over the market and was, when the electricity had not gone out, bathed in the soft and shimmying glow of a large, animated neon sign that towered nearby in the service of a zero-calorie carbonated beverage.

Nadia told Saeed to wait at a short distance, in a darkened alley around the corner, while she unlocked a metal grill door and entered the building alone. Once upstairs she threw a quilt over her bed and pushed her dirty clothes into the closet. She filled a small shopping bag, paused another minute, and dropped it out a window.

The bag landed beside Saeed with a muffled thump. He opened it, found her spare downstairs key, and also one of her black robes, which he furtively pulled on over his own outfit, covering his head with its hood, and then, with a mincing gait that reminded her of a stage-play robber, he approached the front door, unlocked it, and a minute later appeared at her apartment, where she motioned him to sit.

Nadia selected a record, an album sung by a long-dead woman who was once an icon of a style that in her American homeland was quite justifiably called soul, her so-alive but no longer living voice conjuring up from the past a third presence in a room that presently contained only two, and asked Saeed if he would like a joint, to which he fortunately said yes, and which he offered to roll.

WHILE NADIA AND SAEED were sharing their first spliff together, in the Tokyo district of Shinjuku where midnight had already come and gone, and so, technically, the next day had already commenced, a young man was nursing a drink for which he had not paid and yet to which he was entitled. His whiskey came from Ireland, a place he had never been to but evinced a mild fondness for, perhaps because Ireland was like the Shikoku of a parallel universe, not dissimilar in shape, and likewise slung on the ocean-ward side of a larger island at one end of the vast Eurasian landmass, or perhaps because of an Irish gangster film he had gone to see repeatedly in his still-impressionable youth.

The man wore a suit and a crisp white shirt and therefore any tattoos he had or did not have on his arms would not be visible. He was stocky but, when he got to his feet, elegant in his movements. His eyes were sober, flat, despite the drink, and not eyes that attracted the eyes of others. Gazes leapt away from his gaze, as they might among packs of dogs in the wild, in which a hierarchy is set by some sensed quality of violent potential.

Outside the bar he lit a cigarette. The street was bright from illuminated signage but relatively quiet. A pair of drunk salary-men passed him at a safe distance, then an off-the-clock club hostess, taking quick steps and staring at the pavement. The clouds above Tokyo hung low, reflecting dull red back at the city, but a breeze was now blowing, he felt it on his skin and in his hair, a sense of brine and slight chill. He held the smoke in his lungs and released it slowly. It disappeared in the wind's flow.

He was surprised to hear a noise behind him, because the alley to his rear was a cul-de-sac and empty when he came outside. He had examined it, out of habit and quickly, but not carelessly, before turning his back. Now there were two Filipina girls, in their late teens, neither probably yet twenty, standing beside a disused door to the rear of the bar, a door that was always kept locked, but was in this moment somehow open, a portal of complete blackness, as though no lights were on inside, almost as though no light could penetrate inside. The girls were dressed strangely, in clothing that was too thin, tropical, not the kind of clothing you normally saw Filipinas wear in Tokyo, or anyone else at this time of year. One of them had knocked over an empty beer bottle. It was rolling, high-pitched, in a scurrying arc away.

They did not look at him. He had the feeling they did not know what to make of him. They spoke in hushed tones as they passed, their words unintelligible, but recognized by him as *wealthy Tokyo (yakuza?) man.*

Tagalog. They seemed emotional: perhaps excited, perhaps frightened, perhaps both—in any case, the man thought, with women it was difficult to tell. They were in his territory. Not the first time this week that he had seen a group of Filipinos who seemed oddly clueless in his bit of town. He disliked Filipinos. They had their place, but they had to know their place. There had been a half-Filipino boy in his junior high school class whom he had beaten often, once so badly that he would have been expelled, had someone been willing to say who had done it.

He watched the girls walk. Considered.

And slipped into a walk behind them, fingering the metal in his pocket as he went.

IN TIMES OF VIOLENCE, there is always that first acquaintance or intimate of ours, who, when they are touched, makes what had seemed like a bad dream suddenly, evisceratingly real. For Nadia this person was her cousin, a man of considerable determination and intellect, who even when he was young had never cared much for play, who seemed to laugh only rarely, who had won medals in school and decided to become a doctor, who had successfully emigrated abroad, who returned once a year to visit his parents, and who, along with eighty-five others, was blown by a truck bomb to bits, literally to bits, the largest of which, in Nadia's cousin's case, were a head and two-thirds of an arm.

Nadia did not hear of her cousin's death in time to attend the funeral, and she did not visit her relatives, not for lack of emotion but because she wanted to avoid being the cause of unpleasantness. She had planned to go to the graveyard alone, but Saeed had called her and asked through her silences what was the matter, and she had somehow told him, and he had offered to join her, insisted without insisting, which strangely came as a kind of relief. So they went together, very early the following morning, and saw the rounded mound of fresh earth, garlanded with flowers, above her cousin's partial remains. Saeed stood and prayed. Nadia did not offer a prayer, or scatter rose petals, but knelt down and put her hand on the mound, damp from the recent visit of a grave-tender with a watering can, and shut her eyes for a long while, as the sound of a jetliner descending to the nearby airport came and went.

They had breakfast at a café, coffee and some bread with butter and jam, and she spoke, but not of her cousin, and Saeed seemed very present, comfortable being there on that unusual morning, with her not talking of what was most of consequence, and she felt things change between them, become more solid, in a way. Then Nadia went to the insurance company that employed her, handled fleet policies until lunch. Her tone was steady and businesslike. The callers she dealt with only rarely said words that were inappropriate. Or asked her for her personal number. Which, when they did, she would not give.

NADIA HAD BEEN SEEING a musician for some time. They had met at an underground concert, more a jam session really, with perhaps fifty or sixty people crammed into the sound-proofed premises of a recording studio that specialized increasingly in audio work for television—the local music business being, for reasons of both security and piracy, in rather difficult straits. She had, as was by then usual for her, been wearing her black robe, closed to her neck, and he had, as was by then usual for him, been wearing a size-too-small white T-shirt, pinned to his lean chest and stomach, and she had watched him and he had circled her, and they had gone to his place that night, and she had shuffled off the weight of her virginity with some perplexity but not excessive fuss.

They rarely spoke on the telephone and met only sporadically, and she suspected he had many other women. She did not want to inquire. She appreciated his comfort with his own body, and his wanton attitude to hers, and the rhythm and strum of his touch, and his beauty, his animal beauty, and the pleasure he evoked in her. She thought she mattered little to him, but in this she was mistaken, as the musician was quite smitten, and not nearly so unattached to her as she supposed, but pride, and also fear, and also style, kept him from asking more of her than she offered up. He berated himself for this subsequently, but not too much, even though after their last meeting he would not stop thinking of her until his death, which was, though neither of them then knew it, only a few short months away.

Nadia at first thought there was no need to say goodbye, that saying goodbye involved a kind of presumption, but then she felt a small sadness, and knew she needed to say goodbye, not for him, for she doubted he would care, but for her. And since they had little to say to one another by phone and instant message seemed too impersonal, she decided to say it in person, outdoors, in a public place, not at his messy, musky apartment, where she trusted herself less, but when she said it, he invited her up, "for one last time," and she intended to say no but actually said yes, and the sex they had was passionate farewell sex, and it was, not unsurprisingly, surprisingly good.

Later in life she would sometimes wonder what became of him, and she would never know.

THE FOLLOWING EVENING helicopters filled the sky like birds startled by a gunshot, or by the blow of an axe at the base of their tree. They rose, singly and in pairs, and fanned out above the city in the reddening dusk, as the sun slipped below the horizon, and the whir of their rotors echoed through windows and down alleys, seemingly compressing the air beneath them, as though each were mounted atop an invisible column, an invisible breathable cylinder, these odd, hawkish, mobile sculptures, some thin, with tandem canopies, pilot and gunner at different heights, and some fat, full of personnel, chopping, chopping through the heavens.

Saeed watched them with his parents from their balcony. Nadia watched them from her rooftop, alone.

Through an open door, a young soldier looked down upon their city, a city not overly familiar to him, for he had grown up in the countryside, and was struck by how big it was, how grand its towers and lush its parks. The din around him was incredible, and his belly lurched as he swerved.

THREE

NADIA AND SAEED WERE, back then, always in possession of their phones. In their phones were antennas, and these antennas sniffed out an invisible world, as if by magic, a world that was all around them, and also nowhere, transporting them to places distant and near, and to places that had never been and would never be. For many decades after independence a telephone line in their city had remained a rare thing, the waiting list for a connection long, the teams that installed the copper wires and delivered the heavy handsets greeted and revered and bribed like heroes. But now wands waved in the city's air, untethered and free, phones in the millions, and a number could be obtained in minutes, for a pittance.

Saeed partly resisted the pull of his phone. He found the antenna too powerful, the magic it summoned too mesmerizing, as though he were eating a banquet of limitless food, stuffing himself, stuffing himself, until he felt dazed and sick, and so he had removed or hidden or restricted all but a few applications. His phone could make calls. His phone could send messages. His phone could take pictures, identify celestial bodies, transform the city into a map while he drove. But that was it. Mostly. Except for the hour each evening that he enabled the browser on his phone and disappeared down the byways of the internet. But this hour was tightly regulated, and when it ended, a timer would set off an alarm, a gentle, windy chime, as though from the breezy planet of some blue-shimmering science fiction priestess, and he would electronically lock away his browser and not browse again on his phone until the following day.

Yet even this pared-back phone, this phone stripped of so much of its potential, allowed him to access Nadia's separate existence, at first hesitantly, and then more frequently, at any time of day or night, allowed him to start to enter into her thoughts, as she toweled herself after a shower, as she ate a light dinner alone, as she sat at her desk hard at work, as she reclined on her toilet after emptying her bladder. He made her laugh, once, then again, and again, he made her skin burn and her breath shorten with the surprised beginnings of arousal, he became present without presence, and she did much the same to him. Soon a rhythm was established, and it was thereafter rare that more than a few waking hours would pass without contact between them, and they found themselves in those early days of their romance growing hungry, touching each other, but without bodily adjacency, without release. They had begun, each of them, to be penetrated, but they had not yet kissed.

In contrast to Saeed, Nadia saw no need to limit her phone. It kept her company on long evenings, as it did countless young people in the city who were likewise stranded in their homes, and she rode it far out into the world on otherwise solitary, stationary nights. She watched bombs falling, women exercising, men copulating, clouds gathering, waves tugging at the sand like the rasping licks of so many mortal, temporary, vanishing tongues, tongues of a planet that would one day too be no more.

Nadia frequently explored the terrain of social media, though she left little trace of her passing, not posting much herself, and employing opaque usernames and avatars, the online equivalents of her black robes. It was through social media that Nadia ordered the shrooms Saeed and she would eat on the night they first became physically intimate, shrooms still being available for cash-on-demand couriered delivery in their city in those days. The police and anti-narcotic agencies were focused on other, more market-leading substances, and to the unsuspecting, fungi, whether hallucinogenic or portobello, all seemed the ame, and innocuous enough, a fact exploited by a middle-agedocal man with a ponytail who ran a small side business that of-ered rare ingredients for chefs and epicures, and yet was fol-owed and liked in cyberspace mostly by the young.

nape-first with a serrated knife to enhance discomfort, his head-
less body strung up by one ankle from an electricity pylon where
it swayed legs akimbo until the shoelace his executioner used
instead of rope rotted and gave way, no one daring to cut him
down before that.

But even now the city's freewheeling virtual world stood in
stark contrast to the day-to-day lives of most people, to those of
young men, and especially of young women, and above all of
children who went to sleep unfed but could see on some small
screen people in foreign lands preparing and consuming and
even conducting food fights with feasts of such opulence that the
very fact of their existence boggled the mind.

Online there was sex and security and plenty and glamour.
On the street, the day before Nadia's shrooms arrived, there was
a burly man at the red light of a deserted late-night intersection
who turned to Nadia and greeted her, and when she ignored
him, began to swear at her, saying only a whore would drive a
motorcycle, didn't she know it was obscene for a woman to
straddle a bike in that way, had she ever seen anyone else doing

MOHSIN HAMID

42

it, who did she think she was, and swearing with such ferocity that she thought he might attack her, as she stood her ground, looking at him, visor down, heart pounding, but with her grip firm on clutch and throttle, her hands ready to speed her away, surely faster than he could follow on his tired-looking scooter, until he shook his head and drove off with a shout, a sort of strangled scream, a sound that could have been rage, or equally could have been anguish.

THE SHROOMS ARRIVED first thing the following morning at Nadia's office, their uniformed courier having no idea what was inside the package Nadia was signing and paying for, other than that it was listed as foodstuffs. Around the same time, a group of militants was taking over the city's stock exchange. Nadia and her colleagues spent much of that day staring at the television next to their floor's water cooler, but by afternoon it was over, the army having decided any risk to hostages was less than the risk to national security should this media-savvy and morale-sapping spectacle be allowed to continue, and so the building was stormed with maximum force, and the militants were exterminated, and initial estimates put the number of dead workers at probably less than a hundred.

Nadia and Saeed had been messaging each other throughout, and initially they thought they would cancel their rendez-vous planned for that evening, Saeed's second invitation to her home, but when no curfew was announced, much to people's surprise, the authorities perhaps wishing to signal that they were in such complete control that none was needed, both Nadia and Saeed found themselves unsettled and craving each other's company, and so they decided to go ahead and meet after all.

Saeed's family's car had been repaired, and he drove it to Nadia's instead of riding his scooter, feeling somehow less exposed in an enclosed vehicle. But while weaving through traffic his side mirror scraped the door of a shiny black luxury SUV, the conveyance of some industrialist or bigwig, costing more than a house, and Saeed steeled himself for a shouting, perhaps even a beating, but the guard who stepped out of the front passenger-side door of the SUV, assault rifle pointed skyward, merely had time to look at Saeed, a smooth, ferocious glance, before being summoned back in, and the SUV sped off, its owner clearly not wishing, on this night, to tarry.

SAEED PARKED around the corner from Nadia's building, messaged that he had arrived, awaited the thump of the falling plastic bag, slipped into the robe that it contained, and then hurried in and upstairs, much as he had before, except that this time he came bearing bags of his own, bags of barbecued chicken and lamb and hot, fresh-made bread. Nadia took the food from him and put it in her oven so that it might remain insulated and warm—but this precaution notwithstanding, their dinner would be cold when finally eaten, lying there disregarded until dawn.

Nadia led Saeed outside. She had placed a long cushion, its cover woven like a rug, on the floor of her terrace, and she sat on this cushion with her back against the parapet and motioned for Saeed to do the same. As he sat he felt the outside of her thigh, firm, against his, and she felt the outside of his, likewise firm, against hers.

She said, "Aren't you going to take that off?"

She meant the black robe, which he had forgotten he was wearing, and he looked down at himself and over at her, and smiled, and answered, "You first."

She laughed. "Together, then."

"Together."

They stood and pulled off their robes, facing each other, and underneath both were wearing jeans and sweaters, there being a nip in the air tonight, and his sweater was brown and loose and hers was beige and clung to her torso like a soft second skin. He attempted chivalrously not to take in the sweep of her body, his eyes holding hers, but of course, as we know often happens in such circumstances, he was unsure as to whether or not he had succeeded, one's gaze being less than entirely conscious a phenomenon.

They sat back down and she placed her fist on her thigh, palm up, and opened it.

"Have you ever done psychedelic mushrooms?" she asked.

THEY SPOKE QUIETLY under the clouds, glimpsing occasionally a gash of moon or of darkness, and otherwise seeing ripples and churns of city-lit gray. It was all very normal at first, and Saeed wondered if she was perhaps teasing him, or if she had been deceived and sold a dud batch. Soon he had concluded that by some quirk of biology or psychology he was simply, and unfortunately, resistant to whatever it was that mushrooms were supposed to do.

So he was unprepared for the feeling of awe that came over him, the wonder with which he then regarded his own skin, and the lemon tree in its clay pot on Nadia's terrace, as tall as he was, and rooted in its soil, which was in turn rooted in the clay of the pot, which rested upon the brick of the terrace, which was like the mountaintop of this building, which was growing from the earth itself, and from this earthy mountain the lemon tree was reaching up, up, in a gesture so beautiful that Saeed was filled with love, and reminded of his parents, for whom he suddenly felt such gratitude, and a desire for peace, that peace should come for them all, for everyone, for everything, for we are so fragile, and so beautiful, and surely conflicts could be healed if others had experiences like this, and then he regarded Nadia and saw that she was regarding him and her eyes were like worlds.

They did not hold hands until Saeed's perspective had returned, hours later, not to normal, for he suspected it was possible he might never think of normal in the same way again, but to something closer to what it had been before they had eaten these shrooms, and when they held hands it was facing each other, sitting, their wrists resting on their knees, their knees almost touching, and then he leaned forward and she leaned forward, and she smiled, and they kissed, and they realized that it was dawn, and they were no longer hidden by darkness, and they might be seen from some other rooftop, so they went inside and ate the cold food, not much but some, and it was strong in flavor.

SAEED'S PHONE HAD DIED and he charged it in his family's car from a backup battery source he kept in the glove compartment, and as his phone turned on it beeped and chirped with his parents' panic, their missed calls, their messages, their mounting terror at a child not returned safely that night, a night when many children of many parents did not return at all.

Upon Saeed's arrival his father went to bed and in his bedside mirror glimpsed a suddenly much older man, and his mother was so relieved to see her son that she thought, for a moment, she should slap him.

NADIA DID NOT FEEL like sleeping, and so she took a shower, the water chilly because of the intermittent gas supply to her boiler. She stood naked, as she had been born, and put on her jeans and T-shirt and sweater, as she did when alone at home, and then put on her robe, ready to resist the claims and expectations of the world, and stepped outside to go for a walk in a nearby park that would by now be emptying of its early-morning junkies and of the gay lovers who had departed their houses with more time than they needed for the errands they had said they were heading out to accomplish.

LATER THAT DAY, in the evening, Nadia's time, the sun having slipped below her horizon, it was morning in the San Diego, California, locality of La Jolla, where an old man lived by the sea, or rather on a bluff overlooking the Pacific Ocean. The fittings in his house were worn but painstakingly repaired, as was his garden: home to mesquite trees and desert willows and succulent plants that had seen better years, but were still alive and mostly free of blight.

The old man had served in the navy during one of the larger wars and he had respect for the uniform, and for these young men who had established a perimeter around his property, as he watched, standing on the street with their commanding officer. They reminded him of when he was their age and had their strength and their suppleness of movement and their certainty of purpose and their bond with one another, that bond he and his friends used to say was like that of brothers, but was in some ways stronger than that of brothers, or at least than his bond with his own brother, his kid brother, who had passed last spring from cancer of the throat that had withered him to the weight of a young girl, and who had not spoken to the old man for years, and when the old man had gone to see him in the hospital could no longer speak, could only look, and in his eyes was exhaustion but not so much fear, brave eyes, on a kid brother the old man had never before thought of as brave.

The officer didn't have time for the old man but he had time for his age and for his service record, and so he allowed the old man to linger nearby for a while before saying with a polite dip of his head that it would be best if he now moved on.

The old man asked the officer whether it was Mexicans that had been coming through, or was it Muslims, because he couldn't be sure, and the officer said he couldn't answer, sir. So the old man stood silent for a bit and the officer let him, as cars were diverted and told to go some other way, and as rich neighbors who had bought their properties more recently sat at their front windows and stared, and in the end the old man asked how he could help.

The old man felt like a child suddenly, asking this. The officer was young enough to be his grandson.

The officer said they'd let him know, sir.

I'll let you know: that's what the old man's father used to say to him when he was pestering. And in some ways the officer did look like his father, more like his father than like the old man anyway, like his father when the old man was just a boy.

The officer offered to arrange for the old man to be dropped off if he wanted, with kin maybe, or friends.

It was a warm early winter's day, clear and sunny. Far below, the surfers were paddling out in their wetsuits. Above the ocean, in the distance, the gray transport planes were lining up to land at Coronado.

The old man wondered where he should go, and thinking about it, realized he couldn't come up with a single place.

· · ·

AFTER THE ASSAULT on the stock exchange of Saeed and Nadia's city, it seemed the militants had changed strategy, and grown in confidence, and instead of merely detonating a bomb here or orchestrating a shooting there, they began taking over and holding territory throughout the city, sometimes a building, sometimes an entire neighborhood, for hours usually, but on occasion for days. How so many of them were arriving so quickly from their bastions in the hills remained a mystery, but the city was vast and sprawling and impossible to disconnect from the surrounding countryside. Besides, the militants were well known to have sympathizers within.

The curfew Saeed's parents had been waiting for was duly imposed, and enforced with hair-trigger zeal, not just sand-bagged checkpoints and razor wire proliferating but also howitzers and infantry fighting vehicles and tanks with their turrets clad in the rectangular barnacles of explosive reactive armor. Saeed went with his father to pray on the first Friday after the curfew's commencement, and Saeed prayed for peace and Saeed's father prayed for Saeed and the preacher in his sermon urged all the congregants to pray for the righteous to emerge victorious in the war but carefully refrained from specifying on which side of the conflict he thought the righteous to be.

Saeed's father felt as he walked back to campus and his son drove back to work that he had made a mistake with his career, that he should have done something else with his life, because then he might have had the money to send Saeed abroad. Perhaps he had been selfish, his notion of helping the youth and the country through teaching and research merely an expression of vanity, and the far more decent path would have been to pursue wealth at all costs.

Saeed's mother prayed at home, newly particular about not missing a single one of her devotions, but she insisted on claiming that nothing had changed, that the city had seen similar crises before, though she could not say when, and that the local press and foreign media were exaggerating the danger. She did, however, develop difficulties sleeping, and obtained from her pharmacist, a woman she trusted not to gossip, a sedative to take secretly before bed.

At Saeed's office work was slow even though three of his fellow employees had stopped showing up and there ought to have been more to do for those who were still present. Conversations focused mainly on conspiracy theories, the status of the fighting, and how to get out of the country—and since visas, which had long been near-impossible, were now truly impossible for nonwealthy people to secure, and journeys on passenger planes and ships were therefore out of the question, the relative merits, or rather risks, of the various overland routes were guessed at, and picked apart, again and again.

At Nadia's workplace it was much the same, with the added intrigue that came from her boss and her boss's boss being among those rumored to have fled abroad, since neither had returned as scheduled from their holidays. Their offices sat empty behind glass partitions at the prow and stern of the oblong floor—an abandoned suit hanging in its dust cover on a hat rack in one—while the rows of open-plan desks between them remained largely occupied, including Nadia's, at which she was often to be seen on her phone.

NADIA AND SAEED BEGAN to meet during the day, typically for lunch at a cheap burger joint equidistant from their workplaces, with deep booths at the back that were somewhat private, and there they held hands beneath the table, and sometimes he stroked the inside of her thigh and she placed her palm on the zipper of his trousers, but only briefly, and rarely, in the gaps when it appeared waiters and fellow diners were not looking, and they tormented each other in this way, since travel between dusk and dawn was forbidden, and so they could not be alone without Saeed spending the entire night, which seemed to her a step well worth taking, but to him something they should delay, in part, he said, because he did not know what to tell his parents and in part because he feared leaving them alone.

Mostly they communicated by phone, a message here, a link to an article there, a shared image of one or the other of them at work, or at home, before a window as the sun set or a breeze blew or a funny expression came and went.

Saeed was certain he was in love. Nadia was not certain what exactly she was feeling, but she was certain it had force. Dramatic circumstances, such as those in which they and other new lovers in the city now found themselves, have a habit of creating dramatic emotions, and furthermore the curfew served to conjure up an effect similar to that of a long-distance relationship, and long-distance relationships are well known for their potential to heighten passion, at least for a while, just as fasting is well known to heighten one's appreciation for food.

THE FIRST TWO WEEKENDS of the curfew came and went without them meeting, outbursts of fighting making travel first in Saeed's neighborhood and then in Nadia's impossible, and Saeed forwarded to Nadia a popular joke about the militants politely wishing to ensure that the city's population was well rested on their days off. Air strikes were called in by the army on both occasions, shattering Saeed's bathroom window while he was in the shower, and shaking like an earthquake Nadia and her lemon tree as she sat on her terrace smoking a joint. Fighter-bombers grated hoarsely through the sky.

But on the third weekend there was a lull and Saeed went to Nadia's and she met him in a nearby café since it was too risky for her to drop a robe into the street by day, or for him to change outdoors, and so he pulled it on in the café's bathroom while she paid the bill and then with his head covered and eyes on the ground, followed her into her building, and once upstairs and inside they soon slipped into her bed and were nearly naked together and after much pleasure but also what she considered a bit excessive a delay on his part she asked if he had brought a condom and he held her face in his hands and said, "I don't think we should have sex until we're married."

And she laughed and pressed close.

And he shook his head.

And she stopped and stared at him and said, "Are you fucking joking?"

FOR A SECOND Nadia was seized by a wild fury but then as she looked at Saeed he appeared almost lethally mortified and a coil loosened in her and she smiled a little and she held him tight, to torture him and to test him, and she said, surprising herself, "It's okay. We can see."

LATER AS THEY LAY in bed listening to an old and slightly scratched bossa nova LP, Saeed showed her on his phone images by a French photographer of famous cities at night, lit only by the glow of the stars.

"But how did he get everyone to turn their lights off?" Nadia asked.

"He didn't," Saeed said. "He just removed the lighting. By computer, I think."

"And he left the stars bright."

"No, above these cities you can barely see the stars. Just like here. He had to go to deserted places. Places with no human lights. For each city's sky he went to a deserted place that was just as far north, or south, at the same latitude basically, the same place that the city would be in a few hours, with the Earth's spin, and once he got there he pointed his camera in the same direction."

"So he got the same sky the city would have had if it was completely dark?"

"The same sky, but at a different time."

Nadia thought about this. They were achingly beautiful, these ghostly cities—New York, Rio, Shanghai, Paris—under their stains of stars, images as though from an epoch before electricity, but with the buildings of today. Whether they looked like the past, or the present, or the future, she couldn't decide.

THE FOLLOWING WEEK it appeared that the government's massive show of force was succeeding. There were no major new attacks in the city. There were even rumors that the curfew might be relaxed.

But one day the signal to every mobile phone in the city simply vanished, turned off as if by flipping a switch. An announcement of the government's decision was made over television and radio, a temporary antiterrorism measure, it was said, but with no end date given. Internet connectivity was suspended as well.

Nadia did not have a landline at home. Saeed's landline had not worked in months. Deprived of the portals to each other and to the world provided by their mobile phones, and confined to their apartments by the nighttime curfew, Nadia and Saeed, and countless others, felt marooned and alone and much more afraid.

FOUR

THE EVENING CLASS Saeed and Nadia had been taking was finished, having concluded with the arrival of the first dense smogs of winter, and in any case the curfew meant courses such as theirs could not have continued. Neither of them had been to the other's office, so they didn't know where to reach one another during the day, and without their mobile phones and access to the internet there was no ready way for them to reestablish contact. It was as if they were bats that had lost the use of their ears, and hence their ability to find things as they flew in the dark. The day after their phone signals died Saeed went to their usual burger joint at lunchtime, but Nadia did not show, and the day after that, when he went again, the restaurant was shuttered, its owner perhaps having fled, or simply disappeared.

Saeed was aware that Nadia worked at an insurance company, and from his office he called the operator and asked for the names and numbers of insurance companies, and tried phoning them all, one by one, inquiring for her at each. This took time: the telephone company was struggling under the sudden load and also to repair infrastructure destroyed in the fighting, and so Saeed's office landline worked at best intermittently, and when it did, an operator could be swatted out of the swarm of busy tones only rarely, and that operator was—despite Saeed's desperate entreaties, desperate entreaties being common in those days—limited to giving out a maximum of two numbers per call, and when Saeed finally did obtain a new pair of numbers to try, more often than not one or both proved to be nonfunctional on any given day, and he had to ring and ring and ring again.

Nadia spent her lunch hours racing home to stock up on supplies. She bought bags of flour and rice and nuts and dried fruit, and bottles of oil, and cans of powdered milk and cured meat and fish in brine, all at exorbitant prices, her forearms aching from the strain of carrying them up to her apartment, one load after another. She was fond of eating vegetables but people said the key was to have as many calories stashed away as possible, and so foods like vegetables, which were bulky for the amount of energy they could provide, and also prone to spoilage, were less useful. But soon the shelves of shops near her were close to bare, even of vegetables, and when the government instituted a policy that no one person could buy more than a certain amount per day, Nadia, like many others, was both panicked and relieved.

On the weekend she went at dawn to her bank and stood in a line that was already quite long, waiting for the bank to open, but when it opened the line became a throng and she had no choice but to surge forward like everyone else, and there in the unruly crowd she was groped from behind, someone pushing his hand down her buttocks and between her legs, and trying to penetrate her with his finger, failing because he was outside the multiple fabrics of her robe and her jeans and her underclothes, but coming as close to succeeding as possible under the circumstances, applying incredible force, as she was pinned by the bodies around her, unable to move or even raise her hands, and so stunned she could not shout, or speak, reduced to clamping her thighs together and her jaws together, her mouth shutting automatically, almost physiologically, instinctively, her body sealing itself off, and then the crowd moved and the finger was gone and not long afterwards some bearded men separated the mob into two halves, male and female, and she stayed inside the female zone, and her turn at the teller did not come until after lunch, whereupon she took as much cash as was permitted, hiding it on her person and in her boots and putting only a little in her bag, and she went to a money changer to convert some of it into dollars and euros and to a jeweler to convert the remainder to a few very small coins of gold, glancing over her shoulder constantly to make sure she wasn't being followed, and then headed home, only to find a man waiting at the entrance, looking for her, and when she saw him she steeled herself and refused to cry, even though she was bruised and frightened and furious, and the man, who had been waiting all day, was Saeed.

She led him upstairs, forgetting that they might be seen, or not caring, and so not bothering this once with a robe for him, and upstairs she made them both tea, her hands trembling, finding it difficult to speak. She was embarrassed and angry that she was this glad to see him, and felt she might start yelling at him at any moment, and he could see how upset she was and so he silently opened the bags he had brought and gave her a kerosene camping stove, some extra fuel, a large box of matches, fifty candles, and a packet of chlorine tablets for disinfecting water.

"I couldn't find flowers," he said.

She smiled at last, a half-smile, and asked, "Do you have a gun?"

THEY SMOKED A JOINT and listened to music and after a while Nadia tried again to make Saeed have sex with her, not

EXIT WEST

because she felt particularly sexy but because she wanted to cauterize the incident from outside the bank in her memory, and Saeed succeeded again in holding back, even as they pleasured each other, and he told her again that they should not have sex before they were married, that doing otherwise was against his beliefs, but it was not until he suggested she move in with his parents and him that she understood his words had been a kind of proposal.

She stroked his hair as his head rested on her chest and asked, "Are you saying you want to get married?"

"Yes."

"To me?"

"To anyone, really."

She snorted.

"Yes," he said, rising and looking at her. "To you."

She didn't say anything.

"What do you think?" he asked.

She felt great tenderness well up in her for him at that moment, as he waited for her reply, and she felt also a galloping terror, and she felt further something altogether more complicated, something that struck her as akin to resentment.

"I don't know," she said.

He kissed her. "Okay," he replied.

As he was leaving, she saved his office details and he saved hers, and she gave him a black robe to wear, and she told him not to bother stashing it in the crack between her building and the next, where previously he had been hiding the robes he exited in for her to collect, but rather to hold on to it, and she gave him a set of keys too. "So my sister can let herself in next time, if she arrives before me," she explained.

And both of them grinned.

But when he was gone she heard the demolition blows of distant artillery, the unmaking of buildings, large-scale fighting having resumed somewhere, and she was worried for him on his drive home, and she thought it an absurd situation that she would have to wait until she went to work the following day to discover whether he had traversed the distance to his home safely.

Nadia bolted her door and laboriously pushed her sofa against it, so that it was now barricaded from within.

THAT NIGHT, in a rooftop flat not unlike Nadia's, in a neighborhood not far from Nadia's, a brave man stood in the light of a torch built into his mobile phone and waited. He could hear, from time to time, the same artillery that Nadia could hear, though more loudly. It rattled the windows of his flat, but only in a gentle way, without any risk, at present, of them breaking.

The brave man did not have a wristwatch, or a flashlight, so his signal-less phone served both functions, and he wore a heavy winter jacket and inside his jacket were a pistol and a knife with a blade as long as his hand.

Another man had begun to emerge from a black door at the far end of the room, a door black even in the dimness, black despite the beam of the phone-torch, and this second man the brave man watched from his post beside the front door but did nothing visibly to help. The brave man merely listened to the sounds in the stairwell outside, for a lack of sound in the stairwell outside, and stood at his post and held his phone and fingered the pistol inside the pocket of his coat, observing without making any noise.

The brave man was excited, though it would have been difficult to see this in the gloom and in the customary inexpressiveness of his face. He was ready to die, but he did not plan on dying, he planned on living, and he planned on doing great things while he did.

The second man lay on the floor and shaded his eyes from the light and gathered his strength, a knockoff Russian assault rifle by his side. He could not see who was at the front door, just that someone was there.

The brave man stood with his hand on his pistol, listening, listening.

The second man got to his feet.

The brave man motioned with the light of his phone, pulling the second man forward, like a needle-jawed anglerfish might, hunting in the inky depths, and when the second man was close enough to touch, the brave man opened the front door of the flat, and the second man walked through into the quietness of the stairwell. And then the brave man shut the door and stood still once again, biding his time for another.

THE SECOND MAN JOINED the fighting within the hour, among many who would do so, and the battles that now commenced and raged without meaningful interruption were far more ferocious, and less unequal, than what had come before.

War in Saeed and Nadia's city revealed itself to be an intimate experience, combatants pressed close together, front lines defined at the level of the street one took to work, the school one's sister attended, the house of one's aunt's best friend, the shop where one bought cigarettes. Saeed's mother thought she saw a former student of hers firing with much determination and focus a machine gun mounted on the back of a pickup truck. She looked at him and he looked at her and he did not turn and shoot her, and so she suspected it was him, although Saeed's father said it meant nothing more than that she had seen a man who wished to fire in another direction. She remembered the boy as shy, with a stutter and a quick mind for mathematics, a good boy, but she could not remember his name. She wondered if it had really been him, and whether she should feel alarmed or relieved if it had. If the militants won, she supposed, it might not be entirely bad to know people on their side.

Neighborhoods fell to the militants in startlingly quick succession, so that Saeed's mother's mental map of the place where she had spent her entire life now resembled an old quilt, with patches of government land and patches of militant land. The frayed seams between the patches were the most deadly spaces, and to be avoided at all costs. Her butcher and the man who dyed the fabrics from which she had once made her festive clothes disappeared into such gaps, their places of business shattered and covered in rubble and glass.

People vanished in those days, and for the most part one never knew, at least not for a while, if they were alive or dead. Nadia passed her family's home once on purpose, not to speak with them, just to see from the outside if they were there and well, but the home she had forsaken looked deserted, with no sign of inhabitants or life. When she visited again it was gone, unrecognizable, the building crushed by the force of a bomb that weighed as much as a compact automobile. Nadia would never be able to determine what had become of them, but she always hoped they had found a way to depart unharmed, abandoning the city to the predations of warriors on both sides who seemed content to flatten it in order to possess it.

She and Saeed were fortunate that their homes remained for a while in government-controlled neighborhoods, and so were spared much of the worst fighting and also the retaliatory air strikes that the army was calling in on localities thought not merely to be occupied but disloyal.

Saeed's boss had tears in his eyes as he told his employees that he had to shutter his business, apologizing for letting them down, and promising that there would be jobs for them all when things improved and the agency was able to reopen. He was so distraught that it seemed to those collecting their final salaries that they were in fact consoling him. All agreed he was a fine and delicate man, worryingly so, for these were not times for such men.

At Nadia's office the payroll department stopped giving out paychecks and within days everyone stopped coming. There were no real goodbyes, or at least none that she was part of, and since the security guards were the first to melt away, a sort of calm looting, or payment-in-hardware, began, and people left with what they could carry. Nadia hefted two laptop computers in their carrying cases and her floor's flat-screen TV, but in the end she did not take the TV because it would have been difficult to load onto her motorcycle, and passed it instead to a somber-faced colleague who thanked her politely.

ONE'S RELATIONSHIP to windows now changed in the city. A window was the border through which death was possibly most likely to come. Windows could not stop even the most flagging round of ammunition: any spot indoors with a view of the outside was a spot potentially in the crossfire. Moreover the pane of a window could itself become shrapnel so easily, shattered by a nearby blast, and everyone had heard of someone or other who had bled out after being lacerated by shards of flying glass.

Many windows were broken already, and the prudent thing would have been to remove those that remained, but it was winter and the nights were cold, and without gas and electricity, both of which were in increasingly short supply, windows served to take some of the edge off the chill, and so people left them in place.

Saeed and his family rearranged their furniture instead. They placed bookshelves full of books flush against the windows in their bedrooms, blocking the glass from sight but allowing light to creep in around the edges, and they leaned Saeed's bed over the tall windows in their sitting room, mattress and all, upright, at an angle, so that the bed's feet rested on the lintel. Saeed slept on three rugs layered on the floor, which he told his parents suited his back.

Nadia taped the inside of her windows with beige packing tape, the sort normally used to seal cardboard boxes, and hammered heavy-duty rubbish bags into place over them, pounding nails into the window frames. When she had had enough electricity to charge her backup battery, she would lounge around and listen to her records in the light of a single bare bulb, the harsh sounds of the fighting muffled somewhat by her music, and she would then glance at her windows and think that they looked a bit like amorphous black works of contemporary art.

The effect doors had on people altered as well. Rumors had begun to circulate of doors that could take you elsewhere, often to places far away, well removed from this death trap of a country. Some people claimed to know people who knew people who had been through such doors. A normal door, they said, could become a special door, and it could happen without warning, to any door at all. Most people thought these rumors to be nonsense, the superstitions of the feeble-minded. But most people began to gaze at their own doors a little differently nonetheless.

Nadia and Saeed, too, discussed these rumors and dismissed them. But every morning, when she woke, Nadia looked over at her front door, and at the doors to her bathroom, her closet, her terrace. Every morning, in his room, Saeed did much the same. All their doors remained simple doors, on/off switches in the flow between two adjacent places, binarily either open or closed, but each of their doors, regarded thus with a twinge of irrational possibility, became partially animate as well, an object with a subtle power to mock, to mock the desires of those who desired to go far away, whispering silently from its door frame that such dreams were the dreams of fools.

WITHOUT WORK there was no impediment to Saeed and Nadia meeting during the day except for the fighting, but that impediment was a serious one. The few remaining local channels still on the air were saying that the war was going well but the international ones were saying that it was going badly indeed, adding to an unprecedented flow of migrants that was hitting the rich countries, who were building walls and fences and strengthening their borders, but seemingly to unsatisfactory effect. The militants had their own pirate radio station, featuring a smooth-voiced announcer with a deep and unnervingly sexy voice, who spoke slowly and deliberately, and claimed in a decelerated but almost rap-like cadence that the fall of the city was imminent. Whatever the truth, being out and about was risky, so Saeed and Nadia typically met at Nadia's place.

Saeed had once more asked her to move in with him and his family, telling her that he could explain things to his parents, and she could have his room, and he would sleep in the sitting room, and they would not have to marry, they would only, out of respect for his parents, have to remain chaste in the house, and it would be safer for her, for this was no time for anyone to be alone. He had not added that it was especially unsafe for a woman to be alone, but she knew both that he thought it and that it was true, even as she parried his suggestion. He could see that the matter unsettled her, so he did not say it again, but the offer stood, and she considered it.

Nadia was herself coming to acknowledge that this was no longer a city where the risks facing a young woman living independently could be thought of as manageable, and equally importantly she worried for Saeed each time he drove over to see her and back again. But part of her still resisted the idea of moving in with him, with anyone for that matter, having at such great difficulty moved out in the first place, and become quite attached to her small flat, to the life, albeit often lonely, that she had built there, and also finding the idea of living as a chaste half lover, half sister to Saeed in close proximity to his parents rather bizarre, and she might have waited much longer had Saeed's mother not been killed, a stray heavy-caliber round passing through the windshield of her family's car and taking with it a quarter of

Saeed's mother's head, not while she was driving, for she had not driven in months, but while she was checking inside for an earring she thought she had misplaced, and Nadia, seeing the state Saeed and Saeed's father were in when Nadia came to their apartment for the first time, on the day of the funeral, stayed with them that night to offer what comfort and help she could and did not spend another night in her own apartment again.

"A circular quality."
concludes the issue that
it started with.

"robs a bit of the power of
the mother's death."

FIVE

FUNERALS WERE SMALLER and more rushed affairs in those days, because of the fighting. Some families had no choice but to bury their dead in a courtyard or at the sheltered margin of a road, it being impossible to reach a proper graveyard, and so impromptu burial grounds grew up, one extinguished body attracting others, in much the same way that the arrival of one squatter on a disused patch of government land can give rise to an entire slum.

It was customary for a home that had suffered a bereavement to be filled with relatives and well-wishers for many days, but this practice was presently circumscribed by the dangers involved in making a journey in the city, and while people did come to see Saeed's father and Saeed, most came furtively, and could not stay long. It was not the sort of occasion to ask what precisely Nadia's relationship was to the husband and son of the deceased, so no one did, but some did inquire with their glances, and their eyes followed Nadia as she moved around the apartment in her black robe, serving tea and biscuits and water, and not praying, though not ostentatiously not praying, more as if she were busy looking after people's earthly needs and might do so later.

Saeed prayed a great deal, and so did his father, and so did their guests, and some of them wept, but Saeed had wept only once, when he first saw his mother's corpse and screamed, and Saeed's father wept only when he was alone in his room, silently, without tears, his body seized as though by a stutter, or a shiver, that would not let go, for his sense of loss was boundless, and his sense of the benevolence of the universe was shaken, and his wife had been his best friend.

Nadia called Saeed's father "father" and he called her "daughter." This began when they first met, the terms seeming appropriate both to her and to him, and being acceptable forms of address between the young and the old, even when not related, and in any case Nadia had taken one look at Saeed's father and felt him like a father, for he was so gentle, and evoked in her a protective caring, as if for one's own child, or for a puppy, or for a beautiful memory one knows has already commenced to fade.

.   .   .

NADIA SLEPT in what had been Saeed's room, on a pile of carpets and blankets on the floor, having refused Saeed's father's offer to give up his bed, and Saeed slept on a similar though thinner pile in the sitting room, and Saeed's father slept by himself in his bedroom, a room where he had slept for most of his life but where he could not recall the last instance he had slept alone and which for this reason was no longer completely familiar to him.

Saeed's father encountered each day objects that had belonged to his wife and so would sweep his consciousness out of the current others referred to as the present, a photograph or an earring or a particular shawl worn on a particular occasion, and Nadia encountered each day objects that took her into Saeed's past, a book or a music collection or a sticker on the inside of a drawer, and evoked emotions from her own childhood, and jagged musings on the fate of her parents and her sister, and Saeed, for his part, was inhabiting a chamber that had been his only briefly, years ago, when relatives from afar or abroad used to come to visit, and being billeted here again conjured up for him echoes of a better era, and so in these several ways these three people sharing this one apartment splashed and intersected with each other across varied and multiple streams of time.

Saeed's neighborhood had fallen to the militants, and small-scale fighting had diminished nearby, but large bombs still dropped from the sky and exploded with an awesome power that brought to mind the might of nature itself. Saeed was grateful for Nadia's presence, for the way in which she altered the silences that descended on the apartment, not necessarily filling them with words, but making them less bleak in their muteness. And he was grateful too for her effect on his father, whose politeness, when he recalled he was in the company of a young woman, would jar him from what otherwise were interminable reveries and would bring his attention back for a while to the here and now. Saeed wished Nadia had been able to meet his mother, and his mother able to meet her.

Sometimes when Saeed's father had gone to sleep Saeed and Nadia sat together in the sitting room, their sides pressed close for connection and warmth, perhaps holding hands, at most exchanging a kiss on the cheek as a farewell before bed, and often they were silent, but often they spoke in low voices, about how to escape from the city, or about the endless rumors of the doors, or about nothings: the precise color of the refrigerator, the increasingly sorry state of Saeed's toothbrush, the loudness of Nadia's snore when she had a cold.

One evening they were huddled together in this way, under a blanket, in the flickering light of a paraffin lamp, for there was no grid electricity in their part of the city anymore, and no piped gas or water, municipal services having entirely broken down, and Saeed said, "It feels natural to have you here."

"For me too," Nadia replied, resting her head on his shoulder.

"The end of the world can be cozy at times."

She laughed. "Yes. Like a cave."

"You smell a bit like a caveman," she added later.

"And you smell like a wood fire."

She looked at him and felt her body tighten, but she resisted the urge to caress.

When they heard that Nadia's neighborhood had fallen to the militants as well, and that the roads between the two were mostly clear, Saeed and Nadia returned to her flat so she could collect some things. Nadia's building had been damaged, and parts of the wall that faced the street were gone. The backup-battery shop on the ground floor had been looted, but the metal door to the stairway had not been forced, and the overall structure looked more or less sound—in need of substantial repair, certainly, but not on the verge of collapse.

The plastic rubbish bags that covered Nadia's windows were still in place, except for one, which, along with the window itself, had been destroyed, and where the window had formerly been a gash of blue sky was now visible, unusually clear and lovely, except for a thin column of smoke rising somewhere in the distance. Nadia took her record player and records and clothes and food, and her parched but possibly revivable lemon tree, and also some money and gold coins, which she had left hidden in the tree's clay plot, buried within the soil. These items she and Saeed loaded onto the backseat of his family's car, the top of the lemon tree sticking out of a lowered window. She did not remove the money and coins from the pot in case they were searched at a militant checkpoint on the way, which they were, but the fighters who stopped them appeared exhausted and wired and accepted canned supplies as payment to pass.

When they reached home Saeed's father saw the lemon tree and smiled for what seemed like the first time in days. Together the three of them placed it on their balcony, but quickly, because a band of armed men who looked like foreigners had begun to gather on the street below, arguing in a language they could not understand.

NADIA KEPT HER RECORD PLAYER and records out of sight in Saeed's room, even after the customary mourning period for Saeed's mother was over, because music was forbidden by the militants, and their apartment could be searched without warning, indeed it had been once already, militants banging on the door in the middle of the night, and in any case even if she had wanted to play a record there was no electricity, not even enough to charge the apartment's backup batteries.

The night the militants came they were looking for people of a particular sect, and demanded to see ID cards, to check what sort of names everyone had, but fortunately for Saeed's father and Saeed and Nadia their names were not associated with the denomination being hunted. The neighbors upstairs were not so lucky: the husband was held down while his throat was cut, the wife and daughter were hauled out and away.

The dead neighbor bled through a crack in the floor, his blood appearing as a stain in the high corner of Saeed's sitting room, and Saeed and Nadia, who had heard the family's screams, went up to collect and bury him, as soon as they dared, but his body was gone, presumably taken by his executioners, and his blood was already fairly dry, a patch like a painted puddle in his apartment, an uneven trail on the stairs.

The following night, or perhaps the night after that, Saeed entered Nadia's room and they were unchaste there for the first time. A combination of horror and desire subsequently impelled him back each evening, despite his earlier resolution that they do nothing that was disrespectful to his parents, and they would touch and stroke and taste, always stopping short of sex, upon which she no longer insisted, and which they had by now found ample means to circumvent. His mother was no more, and his

father seemed not to concern himself with these romantic matters, and so they proceeded in secret, and the fact that unmarried lovers such as they were now being made examples of and
punished by death created a semi-terrified urgency and edge
to each coupling that sometimes bordered on a strange sort of
ecstasy.

AS THE MILITANTS secured the city, extinguishing the last
large salients of resistance, a partial calm descended, broken by
the activities of drones and aircraft that bombed from the heavens, these networked machines for the most part invisible, and
by the public and private executions that now took place almost
continuously, bodies hanging from streetlamps and billboards
like a form of festive seasonal decoration. The executions moved
in waves, and once a neighborhood had been purged it could
then expect a measure of respite, until someone committed an
infraction of some kind, because infractions, although often al-
leged with a degree of randomness, were invariably punished
without mercy.

Saeed's father went each day to the home of a cousin who
was like an elder brother to Saeed's father and his surviving siblings, and there he sat with the old men and old women and

drank tea and coffee and discussed the past, and they all knew Saeed's mother well and had stories to relate in which she featured prominently, and while Saeed's father was with them he felt not that his wife was alive, for the magnitude of her death impressed itself upon him again with every morning, but rather that he could share some small measure of her company.

Saeed's father tarried at her grave each evening on the way home. Once as he stood there he saw some young boys playing football and this cheered him, and reminded him of his own skill at the game when he was their age, but then he realized that they were not young boys, but teenagers, young men, and they were not playing with a ball but with the severed head of a goat, and he thought, barbarians, but then it dawned upon him that this was the head not of a goat but of a human being, with hair and a beard, and he wanted to believe he was mistaken, that the light was failing and his eyes were playing tricks on him, and that is what he told himself, as he tried not to look again, but something about their expressions left him in little doubt of the truth.

Saeed and Nadia meanwhile had dedicated themselves single-mindedly to finding a way out of the city, and as the overland routes were widely deemed too perilous to attempt, this meant investigating the possibility of securing passage through the doors, in which most people seemed now to believe, especially since any attempt to use one or keep one secret had been proclaimed by the militants to be punishable, as usual and somewhat unimaginatively, by death, and also because those with short-wave radios claimed that even the most reputable international broadcasters had acknowledged the doors existed, and indeed were being discussed by world leaders as a major global crisis.

Following a tip from a friend, Saeed and Nadia headed out on foot at dusk. They were dressed in accordance with the rules on dress and he was bearded in accordance with the rules on beards and her hair was hidden in accordance with the rules on hair, but they stayed in the margins of the roads, in the shadows as much as possible, trying not to be seen while trying not to look like they were trying not to be seen. They passed a body hanging in the air and could hardly smell it until they were downwind, when the odor became almost unbearable.

Because of the flying robots high above in the darkening sky, unseen but never far from people's minds in those days, Saeed walked with a slight hunch, as though cringing a tad at the thought of the bomb or missile one of them might at any moment dispatch. By contrast, because she wanted not to appear guilty, Nadia walked tall, so that if they were stopped and their ID cards were checked and it was pointed out that her card did not list him as her husband, she would be more believable when she led the questioners home and presented the forgery that was supposedly their marriage certificate.

The man they were looking for called himself an agent, though it was unclear if this was due to his specializing in travel or to his operating in secret or to some other reason, and they were to meet him in the labyrinthine gloom of a burnt-out shopping center, a ruin with innumerable exits and hiding places, which made Saeed wish he had insisted Nadia not come and made Nadia wish they had brought a torch or, failing that, a knife. They stood, barely able to see, and waited with mounting unease.

They did not hear the agent approaching—or perhaps he had been there all along—and they were startled by his voice just behind them. The agent spoke softly, almost sweetly, his whisper bringing to mind that of a poet or a psychopath. He instructed them to stand still, to not turn around. He told Nadia to uncover her head, and when she asked why, he said it was not a request.

Nadia had the sense he was extremely close to her, as if he were about to touch her neck, but she could not hear his breathing. There was a small sound in the distance and she and Saeed realized the agent might not be alone. Saeed asked where the door was and where it led to, and the agent replied that the doors were everywhere but finding one the militants had not yet found, a door not yet guarded, that was the trick, and might take a while. The agent demanded their money and Saeed gave it to him, uncertain whether they were making a down payment or being robbed.

As they hurried home, Saeed and Nadia looked at the night sky, at the forcefulness of the stars and the moon's pockmarked brightness in the absence of electric lighting and in the reduced pollution from fuel-starved and hence sparse traffic, and wondered where the door to which they had purchased access might take them, someplace in the mountains or on the plains or by the seaside, and they saw an emaciated man lying on the street who had recently expired, either from hunger or illness, for he did not appear wounded, and in their apartment they told Saeed's father the potential good news but he was oddly silent in response, and they waited for him to say something, and in the end all he said was, "Let us hope."

AS THE DAYS PASSED, and Saeed and Nadia did not hear from the agent again, and increasingly questioned whether they would hear from the agent again, elsewhere other families were on the move. One of these—a mother, father, daughter, son—emerged from the complete blackness of an interior service door.

They were deep inside a vast pedestal floor, below a cluster of blond-and-glass towers filled with luxury apartments and collectively named, by their developer, Jumeirah Beach Residence. On a security camera the family could be seen blinking in the sterile artificial light and recovering from their crossing. They each had a slender build and upright posture and dark skin, and though the feed lacked audio input it was of sufficient resolution that lip-reading software could identify their language as Tamil.

After a brief interlude the family was picked up again by a second camera, traversing a hallway and pushing the horizontal bars that secured a heavy set of double fire-resistant doors, and as these doors opened the brightness of Dubai's desert sunlight overwhelmed the sensitivity of the image sensor and the four figures seemed to become thinner, insubstantial, lost in an aura of whiteness, but they were at that moment simultaneously captured on three exterior surveillance feeds, tiny characters stumbling onto a broad sidewalk, a promenade, along a one-way boulevard on which slowly cruised two expensive two-door automobiles, one yellow, one red, the whining of their revving engines indirectly visible in the way they startled the girl and boy.

The parents held their children's hands and seemed to be at a loss as to which direction to go. Perhaps they were from a coastal village themselves, and not from a city, for they gravitated towards the sea and away from the buildings, and they could be seen at multiple angles following a landscaped pathway through the sand, the parents whispering to one another from time to time, the children eyeing the mostly pale tourists lying on towels and loungers in a state of near-total undress—but in numbers far fewer than normal for the winter high season, though the children could not know this.

A small quadcopter drone was hovering fifty meters above them now, too quiet to be heard, and relaying its feed to a central monitoring station and also to two different security vehicles, one an unmarked sedan, the other a badged van with grilles on its windows, and from the latter vehicle a pair of uniformed men emerged and walked purposefully, but without undue or tourist-alarming haste, along a trajectory that would intersect with that of the Tamil-speaking family in a minute or so.

During this minute the family was also visible in the camera feeds of various tourists' selfie-taking mobile phones, and they seemed to be not so much a cohesive unit but rather four disparate individuals, each behaving in a different way, the mother repeatedly making eye contact with the women she passed and then immediately glancing down, the father patting his pockets and the underside of his backpack as though checking for tears or leaks, the daughter staring at skydivers who were hurtling towards a nearby pier and pulling up at the last moment and landing at a sprint, the son testing the rubberized jogger-friendly surface beneath his feet with each step, and then the minute ended and they were intercepted and led away, apparently bewildered, or overawed, for they held hands and did not resist or scatter or run.

FOR THEIR PART, Saeed and Nadia enjoyed a degree of insulation from remote surveillance when they were indoors, owing to their lack of electricity, but even so their home could still be searched by armed men without warning, and of course as soon as they stepped outside they could be seen by the lenses peering down on their city from the sky and from space, and by the eyes of militants, and of informers, who might be anyone, everyone.

One previously private function they now had to perform in public was the emptying of their bowels, for without piped water the toilets in Saeed and Nadia's building no longer worked. Residents had dug two deep trenches in the small courtyard in the back, one for men and one for women, separated by a heavy sheet on a clothesline, and it was there that all had to squat to relieve themselves, under the clouds, ignoring the stench, face to the ground so that even if the act could be viewed, the identity of the actor might be kept somewhat to oneself.

Nadia's lemon tree did not recover, despite repeated water-

ing, and it sat lifeless on their balcony, clung to by a few desic-
cated leaves.

It might seem surprising that even in such circumstances
Saeed's and Nadia's attitudes towards finding a way out were
not entirely straightforward. Saeed desperately wanted to leave
his city, in a sense he always had, but in his imagination he had
thought he would leave it only temporarily, intermittently, never
once and for all, and this looming potential departure was altogether different, for he doubted he would come back, and the
scattering of his extended family and his circle of friends and
acquaintances, forever, struck him as deeply sad, as amounting
to the loss of a home, no less, of his home.

Nadia was possibly even more feverishly keen to depart, and
her nature was such that the prospect of something new, of
change, was at its most basic level exciting to her. But she was
haunted by worries too, revolving around dependence, worries
that in going abroad and leaving their country she and Saeed
and Saeed's father might be at the mercy of strangers, subsistent
on handouts, caged in pens like vermin.

Nadia had long been, and would afterwards continue to be,
more comfortable with all varieties of movement in her life than
was Saeed, in whom the impulse of nostalgia was stronger, perhaps because his childhood had been more idyllic, or perhaps

because this was simply his temperament. Both of them, though, whatever their misgivings, had no doubt that they would leave if given the chance. And so neither expected, when a handwritten note from the agent arrived, pushed under their apartment door one morning and telling them precisely where to be at precisely what time the following afternoon, that Saeed's father would say, "You two must go, but I will not come."

SAEED AND NADIA SAID this was impossible, and explained, in case of misunderstanding, that there was no problem, that they had paid the agent for three passages and would all be leaving together, and Saeed's father heard them out but would not be budged: they, he repeated, had to go, and he had to stay. Saeed threatened to carry his father over his shoulder if he needed to, and he had never spoken to his father in this way, and his father took him aside, for he could see the pain he was causing his son, and when Saeed asked why his father was doing this, what could possibly make him want to stay, Saeed's father said, "Your mother is here."

Saeed said, "Mother is gone."

His father said, "Not for me."

And this was true in a way, Saeed's mother was not gone for

Saeed's father, not entirely, and it would have been difficult for Saeed's father to leave the place where he had spent a life with her, difficult not to be able to visit her grave each day, and he did not wish to do this, he preferred to abide, in a sense, in the past, for the past offered more to him.

But Saeed's father was thinking also of the future, even though he did not say this to Saeed, for he feared that if he said this to his son that his son might not go, and he knew above all else that his son must go, and what he did not say was that he had come to that point in a parent's life when, if a flood arrives, one knows one must let go of one's child, contrary to all the instincts one had when one was younger, because holding on can no longer offer the child protection, it can only pull the child down, and threaten them with drowning, for the child is now stronger than the parent, and the circumstances are such that the utmost of strength is required, and the arc of a child's life only appears for a while to match the arc of a parent's, in reality one sits atop the other, a hill atop a hill, a curve atop a curve, and Saeed's father's arc now needed to curve lower, while his son's still curved higher, for with an old man hampering them these two young people were simply less likely to survive.

Saeed's father told his son he loved him and said that Saeed must not disobey him in this, that he had not believed in commanding his son but in this moment was doing so, that only death awaited Saeed and Nadia in this city, and that one day when things were better Saeed would come back to him, and both men knew as this was said that it would not happen, that Saeed would not be able to return while his father still lived, and indeed as it transpired Saeed would not, after this night that was just beginning, spend another night with his father again.

SAEED'S FATHER then summoned Nadia into his room and spoke to her without Saeed and said that he was entrusting her with his son's life, and she, whom he called daughter, must, like a daughter, not fail him, whom she called father, and she must see Saeed through to safety, and he hoped she would one day marry his son and be called mother by his grandchildren, but this was up to them to decide, and all he asked was that she remain by Saeed's side until Saeed was out of danger, and he asked her to promise this to him, and she said she would promise only if Saeed's father came with them, and he said again that he could not, but that they must go, he said it softly, like a prayer, and she sat there with him in silence and the minutes passed, and in the end she promised, and it was an easy promise to make because she had at that time no thoughts of leaving Saeed, but it was also a difficult one because in making it she felt she was abandoning the old man, and even if he did have his siblings and his cousins, and might now go live with them or have them come live with him, they could not protect him as Saeed and Nadia could, and so by making the promise he demanded she make she was in a sense killing him, but that is the way of things, for when we migrate, we murder from our lives those we leave behind.

SIX

THEY SLEPT LITTLE that night, the night before their departure from the city, and in the morning Saeed's father embraced them and said goodbye and walked off with moist eyes, but without faltering, the old man thinking it best he leave the young people rather than make them agonize over stepping through the front door with him watching from behind. He would not say where he was going for the day, and so Saeed and Nadia found themselves alone, unable once he was gone to chase him down, and in the quietness of his absence Nadia checked and rechecked the smallish backpacks they would carry, small-ish because they did not want to arouse suspicion, but each full to bursting, like a turtle imprisoned in too tight a shell, and Saeed ran his fingertips over the apartment's furniture and the telescope and the bottle containing the clipper ship, and he also carefully folded a photograph of his parents to keep hidden inside his clothing, along with a memory stick containing his family album, and twice he prayed.

The walk to the rendezvous point was an interminable one, and as they walked Saeed and Nadia did not hold hands, for that was forbidden in public between genders, even for an ostensibly married couple, but from time to time their knuckles would brush at their sides, and this sporadic physical contact was important to them. They knew there was a possibility the agent had sold them out to the militants, and so they knew there was a possibility this was the final afternoon of their lives.

The rendezvous point was in a converted house next to a market that reminded Nadia of her former home. On the ground floor was a dentist's clinic long lacking medicines and painkillers, and as of yesterday lacking a dentist as well, and in the dentist's waiting room they had a shock because a man who looked like a militant was standing there, assault rifle slung over his shoulder. But he merely took the balance of their payment and told them to sit, and so they sat in that crowded room with a frightened couple and their two school-age children, and a young man in glasses, and an older woman who was perched erectly on her seat as though she came from money, even though her clothes were dirty, and every few minutes someone was summoned through to the dentist's office itself, and after Nadia and Saeed were summoned they saw a slender man who also looked like a militant, and was picking at the edge of his nostril with a fingernail, as though toying with a callus, or strumming a musical instrument, and when he spoke they heard his peculiarly soft voice and knew at once that he was the agent they had met before.

The room was gloomy and the dentist's chair and tools resembled a torture station. The agent gestured with his head to the blackness of a door that had once led to a supply cabinet and said to Saeed, "You go first," but Saeed, who had until then thought he would go first, to make sure it was safe for Nadia to follow, now changed his mind, thinking it possibly more dangerous for her to remain behind while he went through, and said, "No, she will."

The agent shrugged as though it was of no consequence to him, and Nadia, who had not considered the order of their departure until that moment, and realized there was no good option for either of them, that there were risks to each, to going first and to going second, did not argue, but approached the door, and drawing close she was struck by its darkness, its opacity, the way that it did not reveal what was on the other side, and also did not reflect what was on this side, and so felt equally like a beginning and an end, and she turned to Saeed and found him staring at her, and his face was full of worry, and sorrow, and she took his hands in hers and held them tight, and then, releasing them, and without a word, she stepped through.

IT WAS SAID in those days that the passage was both like dying and like being born, and indeed Nadia experienced a kind of extinguishing as she entered the blackness and a gasping struggle as she fought to exit it, and she felt cold and bruised and damp as she lay on the floor of the room at the other side, trembling and too spent at first to stand, and she thought, while she strained to fill her lungs, that this dampness must be her own sweat.

Saeed was emerging and Nadia crawled forward to give him space, and as she did so she noticed the sinks and mirrors for the first time, the tiles of the floor, the stalls behind her, all the doors of which save one were normal doors, all but the one through which she had come, and through which Saeed was now coming, which was black, and she understood that she was in the bathroom of some public place, and she listened intently but it was silent, the only noises emanating from her, from her breathing, and from Saeed, his quiet grunts like those of a man exercising, or having sex.

They embraced without getting to their feet, and she cradled

him, for he was still weak, and when they were strong enough
they rose, and she saw Saeed pivot back to the door, as though
he wished maybe to reverse course and return through it, and
she stood beside him without speaking, and he was motionless
for a while, but then he strode forward and they made their way
outside and found themselves between two low buildings, perceiving a sound like a shell held to their ears and feeling a cold
breeze on their faces and smelling brine in the air and they
looked and saw a stretch of sand and low gray waves coming in
and it seemed miraculous, although it was not a miracle, they
were merely on a beach.

The beach was fronted by a beach club, with bars and tables
and large outdoor loudspeakers and loungers stacked away for
winter. Its signs were written in English but also in other Euro-
pean tongues. It seemed deserted, and Saeed and Nadia went
and stood by the sea, the water stopping just short of their feet
and sinking into the sand, leaving lines in the smoothness like
those of expired soap bubbles blown by a parent for a child.
After a while a pale-skinned man with light brown hair came
out and told them to move along, making shooing gestures with
his hands, but without any hostility or particular rudeness, more
as though he was conversing in an international pidgin dialect
of sign language.

They walked away from the beach club and in the lee of a

hill they saw what looked like a refugee camp, with hundreds of tents and lean-tos and people of many colors and hues—many colors and hues but mostly falling within a band of brown that ranged from dark chocolate to milky tea—and these people were gathered around fires that burned inside upright oil drums and speaking in a cacophony that was the languages of the world, what one might hear if one were a communications satellite, or a spymaster tapping into a fiber-optic cable under the sea.

In this group, everyone was foreign, and so, in a sense, no one was. Nadia and Saeed quickly located a cluster of fellow countrywomen and -men and learned that they were on the Greek island of Mykonos, a great draw for tourists in the summer, and, it seemed, a great draw for migrants this winter, and that the doors out, which is to say the doors to richer destinations, were heavily guarded, but the doors in, the doors from poorer places, were mostly left unsecured, perhaps in the hope that people would go back to where they came from—although almost no one ever did—or perhaps because there were simply too many doors from too many poorer places to guard them all.

The camp was in some ways like a trading post in an old-time gold rush, and much was for sale or barter, from sweaters to mobile phones to antibiotics to, quietly, sex and drugs, and there were families with an eye on the future and gangs of young men with an eye on the vulnerable and upright folks and swindlers and those who had risked their lives to save their children and those who knew how to choke a man in the dark so he never made a sound. The island was pretty safe, they were told, except when it was not, which made it like most places. Decent people vastly outnumbered dangerous ones, but it was probably best to be in the camp, near other people, after nightfall.

THE FIRST THINGS Saeed and Nadia bought, Nadia doing the negotiating, were some water, food, a blanket, a larger back-pack, a little tent that folded away into a light, easily portable pouch, and electric power and local numbers for their phones. They found a patch of land at the edge of the camp, partway up the hill, that wasn't too windy or too rocky, and set up their temporary home there, and Nadia felt as she was doing it that she was playing house, as she had with her sister as a child, and Saeed felt as he was doing it that he was a bad son, and when Nadia squatted down beside a scraggly bush and bade him squat down as well, and there concealed tried to kiss him under the open sky, he turned his face away angrily, and then immediately apologized, and placed his cheek against hers, and she tried to relax against him, cheek to bearded cheek, but she was sur-prised, because what she thought she had glimpsed in him in that moment was bitterness, and she had never seen bitterness in him before, not in all these months, not for one second, even when his mother had died, then he had been mournful, yes, depressed, but not bitter, not as though something was corroding his insides. He had in fact always struck her as the opposite of bitter, so quick to smile, and she was reassured when now he held her hand and kissed it, as if making reparations, but she was a bit unsettled too, for it struck her that a bitter Saeed would not be Saeed at all.

They took a nap in the tent, exhausted. When they woke Saeed tried to call his father but an automated message informed him that his call could not be completed, and Nadia tried to connect with people via chat applications and social media, and an acquaintance who had made it to Auckland and another who had reached Madrid replied right away.

Nadia and Saeed sat next to each other on the ground and caught up on the news, the tumult in the world, the state of their country, the various routes and destinations migrants were taking and recommending to each other, the tricks one could gainfully employ, the dangers one needed at all costs to avoid.

In the late afternoon, Saeed went to the top of the hill, and Nadia went to the top of the hill, and there they gazed out over the island, and out to sea, and he stood beside where she stood, and she stood beside where he stood, and the wind tugged and pushed at their hair, and they looked around at each other, but they did not see each other, for she went up before him, and he went up after her, and they were each at the crest of the hill only briefly, and at different times.

As Saeed was coming down from the hill to where Nadia again sat by their tent, a young woman was leaving the contemporary art gallery she worked at in Vienna. Militants from Saeed and Nadia's country had crossed over to Vienna the previous week, and the city had witnessed massacres in the streets, the militants shooting unarmed people and then disappearing, an afternoon of carnage unlike anything Vienna had ever seen, well, unlike anything it had seen since the fighting of the previous century, and of the centuries before that, which were of an entirely different and greater magnitude, Vienna being no stranger, in the annals of history, to war, and the militants had perhaps hoped to provoke a reaction against migrants from their own part of the world, who had been pouring into Vienna, and if that had been their hope then they had succeeded, for the young woman had learned of a mob that was intending to attack the migrants gathered near the zoo, everyone was talking and messaging about it, and she planned to join a human cordon to separate the two sides, or rather to shield the migrants from the anti-migrants, and she was wearing a peace badge on her overcoat, and a rainbow pride badge, and a migrant compassion badge, the black door within a red heart, and she could see as she waited to board her train that the crowd at the station was not the normal crowd, children and older people seemed absent and also there were far fewer women than usual, the coming riots being common knowledge, and so it was likely that people were staying away, but it wasn't until she boarded the train and found herself surrounded by men who looked like her brother and her cousins and her father and her uncles, except that they were angry, they were furious, and they were staring at her and at her badges with undisguised hostility, and the rancor of perceived betrayal, and they started to shout at her, and push her, that she felt fear, a basic, animal fear, terror, and thought that anything could happen, and then the next station came and she shoved through and off the train, and she worried they might seize her, and stop her, and hurt her, but they didn't, and she made it off, and she stood there after the train had departed, and she was trembling, and she thought for a while, and then she gathered her courage, and she began to walk, and not in the direction of her apartment, her lovely apartment with its view of the river, but in the other direction, the direction of the zoo, where she had been intending to go from the outset, and where she would still go, and all this happened as the sun dipped lower in the sky, as it was doing above Mykonos as well, which though south and east of Vienna, was after all in planetary terms not far away, and there in Mykonos Saeed and Nadia were reading about the riot, which was starting in Vienna, and which panicked people originally from their country were discussing online how best to endure or flee.

BY NIGHT IT WAS COLD, and so Saeed and Nadia slept fully dressed, not removing their jackets, and huddled together, wrapped inside their blanket, which was above and around and also below them, providing a degree of cushioning against the hard and somewhat uneven ground. Their tent was too small for them to stand, a long but low pentahedron, in shape like the triangular glass prism Saeed used to have as a child, with which he would refract sunlight into little rainbows. He and Nadia held on to each other at first, cuddling, but cuddling grows uncomfortable after a while, especially in tight quarters, and so eventually they slept back-to-front, initially with him pressed against her from behind, and then, at some later point as the moon passed unseen high overhead, he turned and she turned and she pressed against him.

In the morning when he woke she was watching him and he stroked her hair and she touched his bristles above his lip and below his ear with her finger and he kissed her and things felt good between them. They packed up and Saeed hefted the large backpack and Nadia the tent and they traded one of their small- ish backpacks for a yoga mat that they hoped would make sleep- ing more comfortable.

Without warning people began to rush out of the camp and Saeed and Nadia heard a rumor that a new door out had been found, a door to Germany, and so they ran too, in the middle of the crowd initially, but striding swiftly so they were soon closer to the front. The crowd filled the narrow road and overflowed into the margins and stretched many hundreds of meters at its longest, and Saeed wondered where they were going, and then up ahead he saw they were approaching a hotel or resort of some kind. As they drew nearer he glimpsed a line of men in uniform blocking their way, and he told Nadia, and they were both frightened, and started to slow down, and allow people to pass them, because they had seen in their city what happens when bullets are fired into an unarmed mass of people. But in the end no bullets were fired, the uniformed men simply stopped the crowd and stood their ground, and a few brave or desperate or enterprising souls tried to make it through, running at high speed on either side, where there were gaps, but these few were caught, and after an hour or so the crowd dispersed and most people headed back to the camp.

Days passed like this, full of waiting and false hopes, days that might have been days of boredom, and were for many, but Nadia had the idea that they should explore the island as if they were tourists. Saeed laughed and agreed, and this was the first time he had laughed since they arrived, and it warmed her to see it, and so they carried their loads like trekkers in the wilderness and walked along the beaches and up the hills and right to the edges of the cliffs, and they decided that Mykonos was indeed a beautiful place, and they could understand why people might come here. Sometimes they saw rough-looking groups of men and Saeed and Nadia were careful to keep their distance, and by evening they were always sure to sleep at the periphery of one of the big migrant camps, of which there were many, and to which anyone might belong, joining or leaving as they saw fit.

Once they met an acquaintance of Saeed's and this seemed an almost impossible and happy coincidence, like two leaves blown from the same tree by a hurricane landing on top of each other far away, and it cheered Saeed greatly. The man said that he was a people smuggler, and had helped people escape their city, and was doing the same thing here, because he knew all the ins and outs. He agreed to help Saeed and Nadia, and he cut his rate in half for them and they were grateful, and he took their payment and said he would have them in Sweden by the following morning, but when they woke there was no sign of him. He was gone. He had disappeared overnight. Saeed trusted him and so they stayed where they were for a week, stayed at the same spot in the same camp, but they never saw him again. Nadia knew they had been swindled, such things were common, and Saeed knew it too, but preferred for a while to try to believe that something had happened to the man that had prevented him from returning, and when he prayed Saeed prayed not only for the man's return but also for his safety, until it felt foolish to pray for this man any longer, and after that Saeed prayed only for Nadia and for his father, especially for his father, who was not with them, and should have been. But there was no way back to his father now, because no door in their city went undiscovered by the militants for long, and no one returning through a door who was known to have fled their rule was allowed to live.

One morning Saeed was able to borrow a beard trimmer and trim his beard down to the stubble he had had when Nadia first met him, and that morning he asked Nadia why she still wore her black robes, since here she did not need to, and she said that she had not needed to wear them even in their own city, when she lived alone, before the militants came, but she chose to, because it sent a signal, and she still wished to send this signal, and he smiled and asked, a signal even to me, and she smiled as well and said, not to you, you have seen me with nothing.

. . .

THEIR FUNDS WERE GROWING THINNER, more than half the money with which they had left their city now gone. They better understood the desperation they saw in the camps, the fear in people's eyes that they would be trapped here forever, or until hunger forced them back through one of the doors that led to undesirable places, the doors that were left unguarded, what people in the camps referred to as mousetraps, but which, in resignation, some people were nonetheless trying, especially those who had exhausted their resources, venturing through them to the same place from which they had come, or to another unknown place when they thought anything would be better than where they had been.

Saeed and Nadia began to curtail their wanderings to conserve energy, and thus reduce their need for food and drink. Saeed bought a simple fishing rod, available for a less exorbitant price because its reel was broken and the line had to be spooled out and pulled back in by hand. He and Nadia journeyed to the sea, and stood on a rock, and put bread on the hook, and tried to fish, alone, two people by themselves, all but surrounded by water the breeze was chopping into opaque hillocks, concealing what lay beneath, and they fished and fished for hours, taking turns, but neither of them knew how to fish, or maybe they were just unlucky, and though they felt nibbles, they caught nothing, and it was as though they were merely feeding their bread to the insatiable brine.

Someone had told them the best times to fish were at dawn and dusk, so they stayed out alone longer than they otherwise might have. It was getting dark when they saw four men in the distance, approaching along the beach. Nadia said they should go, and Saeed agreed, and the couple walked away, quickly, but the men seemed to follow, and Saeed and Nadia increased their pace, increased it as much as they could manage, even though Nadia slipped and cut her arm on the rocks. The men were gaining on them, and Saeed and Nadia began to wonder aloud what of their things they could leave behind, to lighten the load, or as an offering that might sate their pursuers. Saeed said perhaps the men wanted the rod, and this seemed more reassuring to them than the alternative, which was to consider what else the men might want. So they dropped the rod, but soon after they rounded a bend and saw a house and outside the house were uniformed guards, which meant the house contained a door to a desirable place, and Saeed and Nadia had never before been relieved to see guards on the island, but they were now. They came close, until the guards shouted at them to stay back, and there Saeed and Nadia stopped, making it clear they would not try to rush the house, sitting down where the guards could see them, and where they felt safe, and Saeed considered whether to run back and retrieve the rod, but Nadia said it was too risky. They both regretted dropping it now. They watched for a while but the four men never appeared, and the two of them set up their tent right there, but were unable to sleep much that night.

THE DAYS WERE GROWING WARMER, and spring was stuttering into being in Mykonos, with buds and scattered flowers. In all the weeks they had been there Saeed and Nadia had never been to the old town, for it was off-limits to migrants at night, and they were strongly discouraged from going there even by day, except to the outskirts, where they could trade with residents, which is to say those who had been on the island longer than a few months, but the gash on Nadia's arm was beginning to fester, and so they had come to the outskirts of the old town to get it tended to at a clinic. A partly shaved-haired local girl who was not a doctor or a nurse but just a volunteer, a teenager with a kind disposition, not more than eighteen or nineteen years of age, cleaned and dressed the wound, gently, holding Nadia's arm as though it was something precious, holding it almost shyly. The two women got to talking, and there was a connection between them, and the girl said she wanted to help

Nadia and Saeed, and asked them what they needed. They said above all they needed a way off the island, and the girl said she might be able to do something, and they should stay nearby, and she took Nadia's number, and each day Nadia visited the clinic and she and the girl spoke and sometimes had a coffee or a joint together and the girl seemed so happy to see her.

The old town was exquisite, white blocks with blue windows scattered along tawny hills, spilling down to the sea, and from the outskirts Saeed and Nadia could spy little windmills and rounded churches and the vibrant green of trees that from a distance looked like potted plants. It was expensive to stay nearby, the camps there often having migrants with more money, and Saeed was becoming worried.

But Nadia's new friend was as good as her word, because very early one morning she put both Nadia and Saeed on the back of her scooter and sped them through still-quiet streets to a house on a hill with a courtyard. They dashed inside and there was a door. The girl wished them good luck, and she hugged Nadia tight, and Saeed was surprised to see what appeared to be tears in the girl's eyes, or if not tears then at least a misty shine, and Nadia hugged her too, and this hug lasted a long time, and the girl whispered something to her, whispered, and then she and Saeed turned and stepped through the door and left Mykonos behind.

SEVEN

THEY EMERGED in a bedroom with a view of the night sky and furnishings so expensive and well made that Saeed and Nadia thought they were in a hotel, of the sort seen in films and thick, glossy magazines, with pale woods and cream rugs and white walls and the gleam of metal here and there, metal as reflective as a mirror, framing the upholstery of a sofa, the switch plate for the lights. They lay still, hoping not to be discovered, but it was quiet, so quiet they imagined they must be in the countryside—for they had no experience of acoustically insulating glazing—and everyone in the hotel must be asleep.

As they stood, though, they saw from their full height what was below the sky, namely that they were in a city, with a row of white buildings opposite, each perfectly painted and maintained and implausibly like the next, and in front of each of these buildings, rising from rectangular gaps in a pavement that was paved with rectangular flagstones, or concrete laid in the manner of flagstones, were trees, cherry trees, with buds and a few white blossoms, as though it had snowed recently and the snow had caught in the boughs and leaves, all along the street, in tree after tree after tree, and they stood and stared at this, for it seemed almost unreal.

They waited for a while but knew they could not stay in this hotel room forever, so eventually they tried the handle of the door, which was unlocked, and emerged into a hallway, leading to a staircase, one flight down which led them to an even grander staircase, off which were floors with more bedrooms but also sitting rooms and salons, and only then did they realize that they were in a house of some kind, surely a palace, with rooms upon rooms and marvels upon marvels, and taps that gushed water that was like spring water and was white with bubbles and felt soft, yes soft, to the touch.

DAWN WAS BREAKING in the city and still they had not been discovered and Saeed and Nadia sat in the kitchen and pondered what to do. The refrigerator was mostly empty, suggesting no one had eaten from it in some time, and while there were boxes and cans of less perishable food in the cupboards, they did not want to be accused of stealing, so they brought their own food out of their backpack and boiled two potatoes for breakfast. They did however take two teabags from the house, and make themselves tea, and each used a spoonful of the house's sugar as well, and if there had been milk in the house they might have helped themselves to a tiny splash of that too, but there was no milk to be found.

They clicked on a television to see if they could discover where they were, and it was soon clear to them that they were in London, and as they watched the television with its intermittently apocalyptic news they felt oddly normal, for they had not watched a television in months. Then they heard a sound from behind them and saw a man was standing there, staring, and they got to their feet, Saeed hefting their backpack and Nadia their tent, but the man turned wordlessly and headed upstairs. They did not know what to make of this. The man had seemed almost as surprised by his surroundings as they were, and they saw no one else until nightfall.

When it was dark people began to emerge from the upstairs room where Nadia and Saeed had themselves first arrived: a dozen Nigerians, later a few Somalis, after them a family from the borderlands between Myanmar and Thailand. More and more and more. Some left the house as soon as they could. Others stayed, staking claim to a bedroom or a sitting room as their own.

Saeed and Nadia picked a small bedroom in the back, one floor up from the ground, with a balcony from which they could jump to the rear garden, if necessary, and from there with luck make an escape.

TO HAVE A ROOM to themselves—four walls, a window, a door with a lock—seemed incredible good fortune, and Nadia was tempted to unpack, but she knew they needed to be ready to leave at any moment, and so she took out of their backpack only items that were absolutely required. For his part Saeed removed the photo of his parents that he kept hidden in his clothing and placed it on a bookshelf, where it stood, creased, gazing upon them and transforming this narrow bedroom, at least partially, temporarily, into a home.

In the hall nearby was a bathroom, and Nadia wanted to take a shower more than anything, more even than she wanted food. Saeed stood watch outside, while she went in and stripped, and observed her own body, leaner than she had ever seen it, and streaked with a grime mostly of her own biological creation, dried sweat and dead skin, and with hair in places from which she had always banished hair, and she thought her body looked like the body of an animal, a savage. The water pressure in the shower was magnificent, striking her flesh with real force, and scouring her clean. The heat was superb too, and she turned it up as high as she could stand, the heat going all the way into her bones, chilled from months of outdoor cold, and the bathroom filled up with steam like a forest in the mountains, scented with pine and lavender from the soaps she had found, a kind of heaven, with towels so plush and fine that when she at last emerged she felt like a princess using them, or at least like the daughter of a dictator who was willing to kill without mercy in order for his children to pamper themselves with cotton such as this, to feel this exquisite sensation on their naked stomachs and thighs, towels that felt as if they had never been used before and might never be used again. Nadia began to put her folded clothes back on but all of a sudden could not bear to, the stench from them was overpowering, and so she was about to wash them in the tub when she heard a banging on the door and realized she must have locked it. Opening up, she saw a nervous and annoyed and dirty-looking Saeed.

He said, "What the hell are you doing?"

She smiled and moved to kiss him, and while her lips did touch his, his did not much respond.

"It's been forever," he said. "This isn't our house."

"I need five more minutes. I have to wash my clothes."

He stared but did not disagree, and even if he had disagreed, she felt a steel in herself which she knew meant she would have washed them anyway. What she was doing, what she had just done, was for her not about frivolity, it was about the essential, about being human, living as a human being, reminding oneself of what one was, and so it mattered, and if necessary was worth a fight.

But the extraordinary satisfactions of the steamy bathroom seemed to have evaporated as she shut the door, and the washing of her clothes, watching the turbid water flow from them down the drain of the bathtub, was disappointingly utilitarian. She tried to recover her former good mood, and not be angry with Saeed, who she told herself was not wrong in his own way, just out of rhythm with her in this moment, and when she emerged from the bathroom wrapped in her towel, her towels, for she had one around her body and another around her hair, and with her dripping but clean clothes in her hands, she was prepared to let the little confrontation between them go.

But he said, looking at her, "You can't stand here like that."

"Don't tell me what I can do."

He looked stung by this comment, and also angry, and she was angry as well, and after he had bathed, and washed his clothes, which he did perhaps as a conciliatory gesture or perhaps because once he was cleansed of his own grime he too realized something of what she had realized, they slept on the slender single bed together without speaking, without touching, or without touching more than the cramped space demanded, for this one night not unlike a couple that was long and unhappily married, a couple that made out of opportunities for joy, misery.

NADIA AND SAEED had crossed over on the morning of a Saturday and by Monday morning when the housekeeper came to work the house was already quite full, home perhaps to fifty squatters, from infants to the elderly, hailing from as far west as Guatemala and as far east as Indonesia. The housekeeper screamed as she unlocked the front door, and the police arrived quickly after, two men in old-fashioned black hats, but they only looked in from outside, and did not enter. Soon there was a vanload more of them, in full riot gear, and then a car with two more who wore white shirts and black vests and were armed with what appeared to be submachine guns, and on their black vests was the word POLICE in white letters but these two looked to Saeed and Nadia like soldiers.

The residents of the house were terrified, most had seen firsthand what the police and soldiers could do, and in their terror they spoke more to one another than they otherwise might, strangers speaking to strangers. A sort of camaraderie evolved, as it might not have had they been on the street, in the open, for then they would likely have scattered, and the devil take the hindmost, but here they were penned in together, and being penned in made them into a grouping, a group.

When the police called over their bullhorns for everyone to exit the house, most agreed among themselves that they would not do so, and so while a few left, the vast majority stayed, Nadia and Saeed among them. The deadline for their departure drew nearer, then nearer still, and then came and went, and they were still there, and the police had not charged, and they felt they had won some kind of a respite, and then something they could never have expected happened: other people gathered on the street, other dark- and medium- and even light-skinned people, bedraggled, like the people of the camps on Mykonos, and these people formed a crowd. They banged cooking pots with spoons and chanted in various languages and soon the police decided to withdraw.

That night it was calm and quiet in the house, though there were sometimes snatches of beautiful singing that could be heard, in Igbo, until quite late, and Saeed and Nadia lay together and held hands on the soft bed in their little back bedroom and were comforted by this, as if by a lullaby, comforted even though they kept their bedroom door locked. In the morning they heard in the distance someone making a call to prayer, at dawn, perhaps over a commandeered karaoke machine, and Nadia was alarmed, waking from a dream and thinking for a second that she was back home in their own city, with the militants, before recalling where she really was, and then she watched, a bit surprised, as Saeed got out of bed and prayed.

ALL OVER LONDON houses and parks and disused lots were being peopled in this way, some said by a million migrants, some said by twice that. It seemed the more empty a space in the city the more it attracted squatters, with unoccupied mansions in the borough of Kensington and Chelsea particularly hard-hit, their absentee owners often discovering the bad news too late to intervene, and similarly the great expanses of Hyde Park and Kensington Gardens, filling up with tents and rough shelters, such that it was now said that between Westminster and Hammersmith legal residents were in a minority, and native-born ones vanishingly few, with local newspapers referring to the area as the worst of the black holes in the fabric of the nation.

But even as people poured into London, some were venturing out of it as well. An accountant in Kentish Town who had been on the verge of taking his own life woke one morning to discover the blackness of a door where the bright entrance to his small but well-lit second bedroom had been. While at first he had armed himself with the hockey stick his daughter had left in his closet, left there along with much else she had abandoned for her gap year, and subsequently he had taken out his phone to call the authorities, he stopped himself to wonder why he was bothering, and proceeded to put away the hockey stick and his phone, and fill his tub as he had planned, and to place the box cutter he had purchased on the little scalloped ledge next to the organic soap his ex-girlfriend would never again use.

He reminded himself that he needed to cut lengthwise if he was serious, up his forearm and not across it, and though he hated the idea of pain, and also of being found naked, he thought this was the right way to go, well considered and well planned. But the nearby blackness unsettled him, and reminded him of something, of a feeling, of a feeling he associated with children's books, with books he had read as a child, or books that had been read to him rather, by his mother, a woman with a gentle lisp and a gentle embrace, who had not died too young but who had deteriorated too young, her illness taking with it her speech, and her personality, and in the process taking his father too, making him into a distant sort of man. And as the accountant thought this, he thought he might step through the door, just once, to see what was on the other side, and so he did.

Later his daughter and his best friend would receive via their phones a photo of him, on a seaside that seemed to have no trees, a desert seaside, or a seaside that was in any case dry, with towering dunes, a seaside in Namibia, and a message that said he would not be returning, but not to worry, he felt something, he felt something for a change, and they might join him, he would be glad if they did, and if they chose to, a door could be found in his flat. With that he was gone, and his London was gone, and how long he remained in Namibia it was hard for anyone who formerly knew him to say.

THE RESIDENTS OF THE HOUSE Nadia and Saeed now occupied wondered if they had won. They savored being indoors, for many had spent many months without a proper roof over their heads, but they knew deep down that a house like this, a palace like this, would not be surrendered so easily, and their relief was therefore fragile.

Nadia experienced the environment of the house as a bit like that of a university dormitory at the start of classes, with complete strangers living in close proximity, many of them on their best behavior, trying to add warmth to conversations and strike poses of friendship, hoping these gestures would become more natural over time. Outside the house much was random and chaotic, but inside, perhaps, a degree of order could be built. Maybe even a community. There were rough people in the house, but there were rough people everywhere, and in life roughness had to be managed. Nadia thought it madness to expect anything else.

For Saeed existence in the house was more jarring. On Mykonos he had preferred the outskirts of the migrant camps, and he had grown accustomed to a degree of independence from their fellow refugees. He was suspicious, especially of the other men around, of whom there were many, and he found it stressful to be packed in so tightly with people who spoke in tongues he did not understand. Unlike Nadia, he felt in part guilty that they and their fellow residents were occupying a home that was not their own, and guilty also at the visible deterioration brought on by their presence, the presence of over fifty inhabitants in a single dwelling.

He was the only one to object when people started to take for themselves items of value in the house, a position that struck Nadia as absurd, and physically dangerous for Saeed besides, and so she had told him not to be an idiot, said it harshly, to protect him rather than to harm him, but he had been shocked by her tone, and while he acquiesced, he wondered if this new way of speaking to one another, this unkindness that was now creeping into their words from time to time, was a sign of where they were headed.

Nadia too noticed a friction between them. She was uncertain what to do to disarm the cycles of annoyance they seemed to be entering into with one another, since once begun such cycles are difficult to break, in fact the opposite, as if each makes the threshold for irritation next time a bit lower, as is the case with certain allergies.

All the food in the house was very quickly consumed. Some residents had money to buy more, but most had to spend their time foraging, which involved going to the depots and stalls where various groups were giving out rations or serving free soup and bread. The daily supplies at each of these were exhausted within hours, sometimes within minutes, and the only option then was to barter with one's neighbors or kin or acquaintances, and since most people had little to barter with, they usually bartered with a promise of something to eat tomorrow or the next day in exchange for something to eat today, a bartering not so much of different goods, exactly, but of time.

ONE DAY Saeed and Nadia were returning home with no food but modestly full bellies, after a reasonably good evening

of foraging, and she was experiencing the peculiar sweet after-
taste and acidity of mustard and ketchup, and Saeed was looking
at his phone, when they heard shouting up ahead and saw people
running, and they realized that their street was under attack by
a nativist mob, Palace Gardens Terrace being roiled in a way
that belied its name. The mob looked to Nadia like a strange and
violent tribe, intent on their destruction, some armed with iron
bars or knives, and she and Saeed turned and ran, but could not
escape.

Nadia's eye was bruised and would soon swell shut and
Saeed's lip was split and kept bleeding down his chin and onto
his jacket, and in their terror they each gripped with all their
might a hand of the other to avoid being separated, but they were
merely knocked down, like many others, and on that evening of
riots across their part of London only three lives were lost, not
many by the recent standards of where they had come from.

In the morning they felt their bed was too tight for them
both, raw as they were from their injuries, and Nadia pushed
Saeed away with her hip, trying to make space, and Saeed
pushed as well, trying to do the same, and for a second she was
angry, and then they turned face-to-face and he touched her
swollen-shut eye and she snorted and touched his swollen-up
lip, and they looked at each other and silently agreed to start
their day without growling.

. . .

AFTER THE RIOTS the talk on the television was of a major operation, one city at a time, starting in London, to reclaim Britain for Britain, and it was reported that the army was being deployed, and the police as well, and those who had once served in the army and the police, and volunteers who had received a weeklong course of training. Saeed and Nadia heard it said that nativist extremists were forming their own legions, with a wink and a nod from the authorities, and the social media chatter was of a coming night of shattered glass, but all this would probably take time to organize, and in that time Saeed and Nadia had to make a decision: whether to stay or to go.

In their small bedroom after sunset they listened to music on Nadia's phone, using the phone's built-in speaker. It would have been a simple matter to stream this music from various websites, but they tried to economize in all things, including the data bundles they had purchased for their phones, and so Nadia downloaded pirated versions whenever she could find them, and they listened to these. She was in any case glad to be rebuilding her music library: from past experience, she did not trust in the continued availability of anything online.

One night she played an album that she knew Saeed liked, by a local band popular in their city when they were in their teens, and he was surprised and happy to hear it, because he was well aware she was not overly fond of their country's pop music, and so it was clear that she was playing this for him.

They sat cross-legged on their narrow bed, their backs propped up by the wall. He extended a hand, palm up on his knee. She took it.

"Let's agree to try harder not to speak shittily to each other," she said.

He smiled. "Let's promise."

"I do."

"I do, as well."

That night he asked her what the life of her dreams would look like, whether it would be in a metropolis or in the country-side, and she asked him whether he could see them settling in London and not leaving, and they discussed how houses such as the one they were occupying might be divided into proper apartments, and also how they might start over someplace else, elsewhere in this city, or in a city far away.

They felt closer on nights when they were making these plans, as though major events distracted them from the more mundane realities of life, and sometimes as they debated their options in their bedroom they would stop and look at each other, as if remembering, each of them, who the other was.

Returning to where they had been born was unthinkable,

and they knew that in other desirable cities in other desirable countries similar scenes must be unfolding, scenes of nativist backlash, and so even though they discussed leaving London, they stayed. Rumors began to circulate of a tightening cordon being put in place, a cordon moving through those of London's boroughs with fewer doors, and hence fewer new arrivals, sending those unable to prove their legal residence to great holding camps that had been built in the city's greenbelt, and concentrating those who remained in pockets of shrinking size. Whether or not this was true there was no denying that an ever more dense zone of migrants was to be found in Kensington and Chelsea and in the adjacent parks, and around this zone were soldiers and armored vehicles, and above it were drones and helicopters, and inside it were Nadia and Saeed, who had run from war already, and did not know where next to run, and so were waiting, waiting, like so many others.

AND YET while all this occurred there were volunteers delivering food and medicine to the area, and aid agencies at work, and the government had not banned them from operating, as some of the governments the migrants were fleeing from had, and in this there was hope. Saeed in particular was touched by a native boy, just out of school, or perhaps in his final year, who came to their house and administered polio drops, to the children but also to the adults, and while many were suspicious of vaccinations, and many more, including Saeed and Nadia, had already been vaccinated, there was such earnestness in the boy, such empathy and good intent, that though some argued, none had the heart to refuse him.

Saeed and Nadia knew what the buildup to conflict felt like, and so the feeling that hung over London in those days was not new to them, and they faced it not with bravery, exactly, and not with panic either, not mostly, but instead with a resignation shot through with moments of tension, with tension ebbing and flowing, and when the tension receded there was calm, the calm that is called the calm before the storm, but is in reality the foundation of a human life, waiting there for us between the steps of our march to our mortality, when we are compelled to pause and not act but be.

The cherry trees exploded on Palace Gardens Terrace at that time, bursting into white blossoms, the closest thing many of the street's new residents had ever seen to snow, and reminding others of ripe cotton in the fields, waiting to be picked, waiting for labor, for the efforts of dark bodies from the villages, and in these trees there were now dark bodies too, children who climbed and played among the boughs, like little monkeys, not because to be dark is to be monkey-like, though that has been and was being and will long be slurred, but because people are monkeys who have forgotten that they are monkeys, and so have lost respect for what they are born of, for the natural world around them, but not, just then, these children, who were thrilled in nature, playing imaginary games, lost in the clouds of white like balloonists or pilots or phoenixes or dragons, and as bloodshed loomed they made of these trees that were perhaps not intended to be climbed the stuff of a thousand fantasies.

One night a fox appeared in the garden of the house where Saeed and Nadia were staying. Saeed pointed it out to Nadia through the window of their little back bedroom, and they were both amazed to see it, and wondered how such a creature could survive in London, and where it had come from. When they asked around if anyone else had seen a fox, all said no, and some people told them it might have come through the doors, and others said it might have wandered in from the countryside, and still others claimed foxes were known to live in this part of London, and an old woman told them they had not seen a fox but rather themselves, their love. They wondered if she meant the fox was a living symbol or the fox was unreal and just a feeling and when others looked they would see no fox at all.

Mention of their love had made Saeed and Nadia a bit uncomfortable, for they had not been very romantic of late, each still perceiving the grating of their presence on the other, and they put this down to being too long in too close proximity, a state of unnatural nearness in which any relationship would suffer. They began to wander separately during the day, and this separation came as a relief to them, though Saeed worried what would happen if the fighting to clear their area began so suddenly that they would not both be able to return home in time, knowing from experience that a mobile phone could be a fickle connection, its signal thought in normal circumstances to be like the sunlight or the moonlight, but in actuality capable of an instant and endless eclipse, and Nadia worried about the promise she had made Saeed's father, whom she too had called father, to stay with Saeed until he was safe, worried what it would make her to be proven untrue to this promise, and whether that would mean she stood for nothing whatsoever.

But liberated from claustrophobic closeness by day, exploring apart, they converged with more warmth at night, even if sometimes this warmth felt like that between relatives rather than between lovers. They began to sit on the balcony outside their bedroom and wait in the dark for the fox to appear below, in the garden. Such a noble animal, noble though it was fond of rummaging in the trash.

As they sat they would on occasion hold hands, and on occasion kiss, and once in a while feel the rekindling of an otherwise diminished fire and go to their bed and torment each other's bodies, never having sex, but never needing to, not anymore, following a different ritual that still resulted in release. Then they would sleep, or if not sleepy go back onto the balcony and wait for the fox, and the fox was unpredictable, it might come and it might not, but often it did, and when it did they were relieved, for it meant the fox had not disappeared and had not been killed and had not found another part of town to make home. One night the fox encountered a soiled diaper, pulled it out of the trash and sniffed at it, as if wondering what it was, and then dragged it around the garden, fouling the grass, changing course again and again, like a pet dog with a toy, or a bear with an unfortunate hunter in its maw, in any case moving with both design and unpredictable wildness, and when it was done the diaper lay in shreds.

That night the electricity went out, cut off by the authorities, and Kensington and Chelsea descended into darkness. A sharp fear descended also, and the call to prayer they had often heard in the distance from the park was silenced. They supposed the karaoke player that might have been used for that task was unable to run on batteries.

EIGHT

THE COMPLEXITIES of London's electricity network were such that a few motes of nighttime brightness remained in Saeed and Nadia's locality, at properties on the edges, near where barricades and checkpoints were manned by armed government forces, and in scattered pockets that were for some reason difficult to disconnect, and in the odd building here and there where an enterprising migrant had rigged together a connection to a still-active high-voltage line, risking and in some cases succumbing to electrocution. Overwhelmingly, though, around Saeed and Nadia it was dark.

Mykonos had not been well lit, but electricity had reached everywhere there were wires. In their own fled city, when the electricity had gone, it had gone for all. But in London there were parts as bright as ever, brighter than anyplace Saeed or Nadia had seen before, glowing up into the sky and reflecting down again from the clouds, and in contrast the city's dark swaths seemed darker, more significant, the way that blackness in the ocean suggests not less light from above, but a sudden drop-off in the depths below.

From dark London, Saeed and Nadia wondered what life must be like in light London, where they imagined people dined in elegant restaurants and rode in shiny black cabs, or at least went to work in offices and shops and were free to journey about as they pleased. In dark London, rubbish accrued, uncollected, and underground stations were sealed. The trains kept running, skipping stops near Saeed and Nadia but felt as a rumble beneath their feet and heard at a low, powerful frequency, almost subsonic, like thunder or the detonation of a massive, distant bomb.

At night, in the darkness, as drones and helicopters and surveillance balloons prowled intermittently overhead, fights would sometimes break out, and there were murders and rapes and assaults as well. Some in dark London blamed these incidents on nativist provocateurs. Others blamed other migrants, and began to move, in the manner of cards dealt from a shuffled deck during the course of a game, reassembling themselves in suits and runs of their own kind, like with like, or rather superficially like with superficially like, all the hearts together, all the clubs together, all the Sudanese, all the Hondurans.

Saeed and Nadia did not move, but their house began to change nonetheless. Nigerians were initially the largest among many groups of residents, but every so often a non-Nigerian family would relocate out of the house, and their place would almost always be taken by more Nigerians, and so the house began to be known as a Nigerian house, like the two on either side. The elder Nigerians of these three houses would meet in the garden of the property to the right of Saeed and Nadia's, and this meeting they called the council. Women and men both attended, but the only obvious non-Nigerian who attended was Nadia.

The first time Nadia went the others seemed surprised to see her, not merely because of her ethnicity but because of her relatively young age. Momentarily there was a silence, but then an old woman with a turban who lived with her daughter and grandsons in the bedroom above Saeed and Nadia's, and whom Nadia had helped on more than one occasion to ascend the stairs, the old woman being regal in posture but also quite large, this old woman motioned to Nadia, beckoned Nadia to come stand at her side, to stand beside the garden chair on which she was sitting. This seemed to settle the matter, and Nadia was not questioned or asked to leave.

Initially Nadia did not follow much of what was being said, just snippets here and there, but over time she understood more and more, and she understood also that the Nigerians were in fact not all Nigerians, some were half Nigerians, or from places that bordered Nigeria, from families that spanned both sides of a border, and further that there was perhaps no such thing as a Nigerian, or certainly no one common thing, for different Nigerians spoke different tongues among themselves, and belonged to different religions. Together in this group they conversed in a language that was built in large part from English, but not solely from English, and some of them were in any case more familiar with English than were others. Also they spoke different variations of English, different Englishes, and so when Nadia gave voice to an idea or opinion among them, she did not need to fear that her views could not be comprehended, for her English was like theirs, one among many.

The activities of the council were mundane, making decisions on room disputes or claims of theft or unneighborly behavior, and also on relations with other houses on the street. Deliberations were often slow and cumbersome, so these gatherings were not particularly thrilling. And yet Nadia looked forward to them. They represented something new in her mind, the birth of something new, and she found these people who were both like and unlike those she had known in her city, familiar and unfamiliar, she found them interesting, and she found their seeming acceptance of her, or at least tolerance of her, rewarding, an achievement in a way.

Among the younger Nigerians Nadia acquired a bit of a special status, perhaps because they saw her with their elders, or perhaps because of her black robe, and so the younger Nigerian men and women and the older Nigerian boys and girls, the ones who often had quick jibes to make about many of the others in the house, rarely said anything of that nature to her, or about her, at least in her presence. She came and went unruffled through the crowded rooms and passages, unruffled except by a fast-talking Nigerian woman her own age, a woman with a leather jacket and a chipped tooth, who stood like a gunslinger, with hips open and belt loose and hands at her sides, and spared no one from her verbal lashings, from her comments that would follow you even as you passed her and left her behind.

Saeed, though, was less comfortable. As he was a young man the other young men would size him up from time to time, as young men do, and Saeed found this disconcerting. Not because he had not encountered anything similar in his own country, he had, but because here in this house he was the only man from his country, and those sizing him up were from another country, and there were far more of them, and he was alone. This touched upon something basic, something tribal, and evoked tension and a sort of suppressed fear. He was uncertain when he could relax, if he could relax, and so when he was outside his bedroom but inside the house he seldom felt fully at ease.

Once, he was alone, arriving home while Nadia was at a meeting of the council, and the woman in the leather jacket stood in the hall, blocking his way with her narrow, jagged form, her back leaning against one wall, a foot planted on the other. Saeed did not like to admit it but he was intimidated by her, by her intensity and by the speed and unpredictability of her words, words that he often could not understand, but words that made others laugh. He stood there and waited for her to move, to yield space for him to pass. But she did not move, and so he said excuse me, and she said why should I excuse you, she said more than that, but all he could catch was that phrase. Saeed was angry that she was toying with him, and alarmed also, and he considered turning around and coming back later. But he realized at that moment that there was a man behind him, a tough-looking Nigerian man. Saeed had heard that this man had a gun, though he could not see it on him, but many of the migrants in dark London had taken to carrying knives and other weapons, being as they were in a state of siege, and liable to be attacked by government forces at any time, or in some cases being predisposed to carrying weapons, having done it where they came from, and so continuing to do it here, which Saeed suspected was the case with this man.

Saeed wanted to run but had nowhere to run to, and tried to hide his panic, but then the woman in the leather jacket removed her foot from the wall, and there was space for Saeed to pass, and so he squeezed through, brushing her body with his, and feeling emasculated as he did so, and when he was alone in his and Nadia's room he sat on the bed and his heart was racing and he wanted to shout and to huddle in a corner but of course he did neither.

AROUND A BEND, on Vicarage Gate, was a house known to be a house of people from his country. Saeed began to spend more time there, drawn by the familiar languages and accents and the familiar smell of the cooking. One afternoon he was there at prayer time, and he joined his fellow countrymen in prayer in the back garden, under a blue sky that seemed shockingly blue, like the sky of another world, absent the airborne dust of the city where he had spent his entire life, and also peering out into space from a higher latitude, a different perch on the spinning Earth, nearer its pole than its equator, and so glimpsing the void from a different angle, a bluer angle, and as he

MOHSIN HAMID

prayed he felt praying was different here, somehow, in the garden of this house, with these men. It made him feel part of something, not just something spiritual, but something human, part
of this group, and for a wrenchingly painful second he thought
of his father, and then a bearded man with two white marks in
the black on either side of his chin, marks like those of a great cat
or wolf, put his arm around Saeed and said brother would you
like some tea.

That day Saeed felt he was really accepted by this house, and
he thought he could ask the man with the white-marked beard if
there was space there for him and Nadia, whom he called his
wife. The man said there was always space for a brother and
sister, though sadly not a room they could share, but Saeed could
stay with him and some other men on the floor of the living
room, provided that is he did not mind sleeping on the floor, and
Nadia could stay upstairs with the women, unfortunately even
he and his own wife were split up in this manner, and they were
among the first residents, but it was the only civilized way to
cram as many people into the house as they had managed to do,
as was righteous to do.

When Saeed told Nadia this good news she did not act like it
was good news at all.

"Why would we want to move?" she said.

152

"To be among our own kind," Saeed answered.

"What makes them our kind?"

"They're from our country."

"From the country we used to be from."

"Yes." Saeed tried not to sound annoyed.

"We've left that place."

"That doesn't mean we have no connection."

"They're not like me."

"You haven't met them."

"I don't need to." She released a long, taut breath. "Here we have our own room," she said, softening her tone. "Just the two of us. It's a big luxury. Why would we give that up to sleep apart? Among dozens of strangers?"

Saeed had no answer for this. Considering it later, he thought it was indeed odd that he would want to give up their bedroom for a pair of separated spaces, with a barrier between them, as when they lived in his parents' home, a time he now thought of fondly in a way, despite the horrors, fondly in terms of how he had felt for Nadia and she had felt for him, how they had felt together. He did not press the point, but when Nadia brought her face close to his in bed that night, close enough to tickle his lips with her breathing, he was unable to muster the enthusiasm to bridge the tiny distance it would have taken to kiss.

. . .

EVERY DAY A FLIGHT of fighter aircraft would streak through the sky, screaming a reminder to the people of dark London of the technological superiority of their opponents, of the government and nativist forces. At the borders of their locality Saeed and Nadia could occasionally glimpse tanks and armored vehicles and communication arrays and robots that walked or crawled like animals, bearing loads for soldiers or rehearsing the disarming of explosives or perhaps preparing to do some other unknown task. Even more than the fighter planes and the tanks these robots, few though they were, and the drones overhead, were frightening, because they suggested an unstoppable efficiency, an inhuman power, and evoked the kind of dread that a small mammal feels before a predator of an altogether different order, like a rodent before a snake.

In meetings of the council Nadia listened as the elders discussed what to do when the operation finally came. All agreed that the most important thing was to manage the impetuousness of the youngsters, for armed resistance would likely lead to a slaughter, and nonviolence was surely their most potent response, shaming their attackers into civility. All agreed on this except Nadia, who was unsure what she thought, who had seen what happens to people who surrender, as her former city surrendered to the militants, and who thought that the young people with their guns and their knives and their fists and their teeth were entitled to use these things, and that the ferocity of the little was sometimes all that kept them safe from the predations of the big. But there was wisdom in what the elders said too, and so she was unsure.

Saeed also was unsure. But in the nearby house of his fellow countryfolk the man with the white-marked beard spoke of martyrdom, not as the most desirable outcome but as one possible end of a path the right-minded had no other choice but to follow, and advocated a banding together of migrants along religious principles, cutting across divisions of race or language or nation, for what did those divisions matter now in a world full of doors, the only divisions that mattered now were between those who sought the right of passage and those who would deny them passage, and in such a world the religion of the righteous must defend those who sought passage. Saeed was torn because he was moved by these words, strengthened by them, and they were not the barbarous words of the militants back home, the militants because of whom his mother was dead, and possibly by now his father as well, but at the same time the gathering of men drawn to the words of the man with the white-marked beard sporadically did remind him of the militants, and when he thought this he felt something rancid in himself, like he was rotting from within.

There were guns in the house of his fellow countryfolk, more arriving each day through the doors. Saeed accepted a pistol but not a rifle, since he could conceal it, and in his heart he would not have been able to say if he took the pistol because it would make him safer from the nativists or from the Nigerians, his own neighbors. As he undressed that night he did not speak of it, but also he did not hide it from Nadia, and upon seeing the pistol he thought she would fight with him, or at least argue, for he knew what the council had decided. But she did not do so.

Instead she watched him, and he looked at her, and he saw her animal form, the strangeness of her face and her body, and she saw the strangeness of his, and when he reached for her she came to him, came to him though she moved slightly away, and there was a mutual violence and excitement to their coupling, a kind of shocked, almost painful surprise.

Only after Nadia had fallen asleep and Saeed lay there in the moonlight that crept between and around the blinds did he consider that he had no idea how to use or maintain a pistol, not the faintest clue, beyond the fact that pulling the trigger should make it fire. He realized he was being ridiculous, and must return it the very next day.

. . .

A THRIVING TRADE in electricity was under way in dark London, run by those who lived in pockets with power, and Saeed and Nadia were able to recharge their phones from time to time, and if they walked at the edges of their locality they could pick up a strong signal, and so like many others they caught up with the world in this way, and once as Nadia sat on the steps of a building reading the news on her phone across the street from a detachment of troops and a tank she thought she saw online a photograph of herself sitting on the steps of a building reading the news on her phone across the street from a detachment of troops and a tank, and she was startled, and wondered how this could be, how she could both read this news and be this news, and how the newspaper could have published this image of her instantaneously, and she looked about for a photographer, and she had the bizarre feeling of time bending all around her, as though she was from the past reading about the future, or from the future reading about the past, and she almost felt that if she got up and walked home at this moment there would be two Nadias, that she would split into two Nadias, and one would stay on the steps reading and one would walk home, and two different lives would unfold for these two different selves, and she thought she was losing her balance, or possibly her mind, and then she zoomed in on the image and saw that the woman in the black robe reading the news on her phone was actually not her at all.

The news in those days was full of war and migrants and nativists, and it was full of fracturing too, of regions pulling away from nations, and cities pulling away from hinterlands, and it seemed that as everyone was coming together everyone was also moving apart. Without borders nations appeared to be becoming somewhat illusory, and people were questioning what role they had to play. Many were arguing that smaller units made more sense, but others argued that smaller units could not defend themselves.

Reading the news at that time one was tempted to conclude that the nation was like a person with multiple personalities, some insisting on union and some on disintegration, and that this person with multiple personalities was furthermore a person whose skin appeared to be dissolving as they swam in a soup full of other people whose skins were likewise dissolving. Even Britain was not immune from this phenomenon, in fact some said Britain had already split, like a man whose head had been chopped off and yet still stood, and others said Britain was an island, and islands endure, even if the people who come to them change, and so it had been for millennia, and so it would be for millennia more.

The fury of those nativists advocating wholesale slaughter was what struck Nadia most, and it struck her because it seemed so familiar, so much like the fury of the militants in her own city. She wondered whether she and Saeed had done anything by moving, whether the faces and buildings had changed but the basic reality of their predicament had not.

But then around her she saw all these people of all these different colors in all these different attires and she was relieved, better here than there she thought, and it occurred to her that she had been stifled in the place of her birth for virtually her entire life, that its time for her had passed, and a new time was here, and, fraught or not, she relished this like the wind in her face on a hot day when she rode her motorcycle and lifted the visor of her helmet and embraced the dust and the pollution and the little bugs that sometimes went into your mouth and made you recoil and even spit, but after spitting grin, and grin with a wildness.

FOR OTHERS TOO the doors came as a release. In the hills above Tijuana was an orphanage called simply the House of the Children, perhaps because it was not precisely an orphanage. Or not only an orphanage, though that is what it was referred to by the college students from across the border who would sometimes come here to do volunteer work: painting, carpentry, the hanging and spackling of drywall. But many of the children in the House of the Children had at least one living parent or sibling or uncle or aunt. Usually these relatives labored on the other side, in the United States, and their absences would last until the child was old enough to attempt the crossing, or until the relative was exhausted enough to return, or on occasion, quite often, forever, because life and its end are unpredictable, especially at a distance, where death seems to operate with such whimsical aim.

The House sat on a ridge at the crest of a hill, fronting a street. Its chain-link-fenced and partly concrete-floored play area was at the back, facing a parched valley, on which the other low dwellings of that street also opened, some of them rising on stilts, as though jutting out to sea, an effect that was incongruous, given the dryness and lack of water all about. But the Pacific Ocean was only a couple hours' walk to the west, and besides, stilts made sense given the terrain.

Out of a black door in a nearby cantina, admittedly an atypical place for a young woman like herself to be found, a young woman was emerging. The owner made no fuss over it, for the times were such, and once this young woman had emerged she rose and strode to the orphanage. There she located another young woman, or rather a grown girl, and the young woman hugged the girl, whom she recognized only because she had seen her on electronic displays, on the screens of phones and computers, it having been that many years, and the girl hugged her mother and then became shy.

The girl's mother met the adults who ran the orphanage, and many of the children, who stared at her and chattered as though she was a sign of something, which of course she was, since if she had come then others would come too. Dinner that evening was rice and refried beans served on paper plates, eaten on an unbroken row of tables flanked by benches, and the mother sat at the center, like a dignitary or a holy figure, and told stories that some of the children, being children, imagined happening to their own mothers, now, or before, when their mothers were still alive.

The mother who had returned on this day spent the night at the orphanage so her daughter could say her farewells. And then mother and daughter walked together to the cantina, and the owner allowed them in, shaking his head but smiling as well, the smile bending his mustache, and making his fierce visage somewhat goofy for a moment, and with that the mother and her daughter were gone.

IN LONDON, Saeed and Nadia heard that military and paramilitary formations had fully mobilized and deployed in the city from all over the country. They imagined British regiments with ancient names and modern kit standing ready to cut through any resistance that might be encountered. A great massacre, it seemed, was in the offing. Both of them knew that the battle of London would be hopelessly one-sided, and like many others they no longer ventured far from their home.

The operation to clear the migrant ghetto in which Saeed and Nadia found themselves began badly, with a police officer shot in the leg within seconds as his unit moved into an occupied cinema near Marble Arch, and then the flat sounds of a firefight commenced, coming from there but also from elsewhere, growing and growing, all around, and Saeed, who was caught in the open, ran back to the house, and found the heavy front door locked shut, and he banged on it until it opened, Nadia yanking him in and slamming it behind him.

They went to their room in the back and pushed their mattress up against the window and sat together in one corner and waited. They heard helicopters and more shooting and announcements to peacefully vacate the area made over speakers so powerful that they shook the floor, and they saw through the gap between mattress and window thousands of leaflets dropping from the sky, and after a while they saw smoke and smelled burning, and then it was quiet, but the smoke and the smell lasted a long time, particularly the smell, lingering even when the wind direction changed.

That night a rumor spread that over two hundred migrants had been incinerated when the cinema burned down, children and women and men, but especially children, so many children, and whether or not this was true, or any of the other rumors, of a bloodbath in Hyde Park, or in Earl's Court, or near the Shepherd's Bush roundabout, migrants dying in their scores, whatever it was that had happened, something seemed to have happened, for there was a pause, and the soldiers and police officers and volunteers who had advanced into the outer edges of the ghetto pulled back, and there was no more shooting that night.

The next day was quiet, and the day after that, and on the second day of quiet Saeed and Nadia removed the mattress from their window and dared to venture outside and forage for food but there was none to be found. The depots and soup kitchens were shut. Some supplies were coming through the doors, but not nearly enough. The council met and requisitioned all provisions in the three houses, and these were rationed, with most going to the children, and Saeed and Nadia getting a handful of almonds each one day, and a tin of herring to share the next.

THEY SAT ON THEIR BED and watched the rain and talked as they often did about the end of the world, and Saeed wondered aloud once again if the natives would really kill them, and

Nadia said once again that the natives were so frightened that they could do anything.

"I can understand it," she said. "Imagine if you lived here. And millions of people from all over the world suddenly arrived."

"Millions arrived in our country," Saeed replied. "When there were wars nearby."

"That was different. Our country was poor. We didn't feel we had as much to lose."

Outside on the balcony the rain clattered in pots and pans, and periodically Saeed or Nadia would get up and open the window and carry two of these to the bathroom and empty them into the stoppered tub, which the council had designated part of the house's emergency water supply, now that the taps had run dry.

Nadia watched Saeed and not for the first time wondered if she had led him astray. She thought maybe he had in the end been wavering about leaving their city, and she thought maybe she could have tipped him either way, and she thought he was basically a good and decent man, and she was filled with compassion for him in that instant, as she observed his face with its gaze upon the rain, and she realized she had not in her life felt so strongly for anyone in the world as she had for Saeed in the moments of those first months when she had felt most strongly for him.

Saeed for his part wished he could do something for Nadia, could protect her from what would come, even if he understood, at some level, that to love is to enter into the inevitability of one day not being able to protect what is most valuable to you. He thought she deserved better than this, but he could see no way out, for they had decided not to run, not to play roulette with yet another departure. To flee forever is beyond the capacity of most: at some point even a hunted animal will stop, exhausted, and await its fate, if only for a while.

"What do you think happens when you die?" Nadia asked him.

"You mean the afterlife?"

"No, not after. When. In the moment. Do things just go black, like a phone screen turning off? Or do you slip into something strange in the middle, like when you're falling asleep, and you're both here and there?"

Saeed thought that it depended on how you died. But he saw Nadia seeing him, so intent on his answer, and he said, "I think it would be like falling asleep. You'd dream before you were gone."

It was all the protection he could offer her then. And she smiled at this, a warm, bright smile, and he wondered if she believed him or if she thought, no, dearest, that is not what you think at all.

.   .   .

BUT A WEEK PASSED. And then another. And then the natives and their forces stepped back from the brink.

Perhaps they had decided they did not have it in them to do what would have needed to be done, to corral and bloody and where necessary slaughter the migrants, and had determined that some other way would have to be found. Perhaps they had grasped that the doors could not be closed, and new doors would continue to open, and they had understood that the denial of coexistence would have required one party to cease to exist, and the extinguishing party too would have been transformed in the process, and too many native parents would not after have been able to look their children in the eye, to speak with head held high of what their generation had done. Or perhaps the sheer number of places where there were now doors had made it useless to fight in any one.

And so, irrespective of the reason, decency on this occasion won out, and bravery, for courage is demanded not to attack when afraid, and the electricity and water came on again, and negotiations ensued, and word spread, and among the cherry trees on Palace Gardens Terrace Saeed and Nadia and their neighbors celebrated, they celebrated long into the night.

NINE

THAT SUMMER it seemed to Saeed and Nadia that the whole planet was on the move, much of the global south headed to the global north, but also southerners moving to other southern places and northerners moving to other northern places. In the formerly protected greenbelt around London a ring of new cities was being built, cities that would be able to accommodate more people again than London itself. This development was called the London Halo, one of innumerable human halos and satellites and constellations springing up in the country and in the world.

It was here that Saeed and Nadia found themselves in those warmer months, in one of the worker camps, laboring away. In exchange for their labor in clearing terrain and building infrastructure and assembling dwellings from prefabricated blocks, migrants were promised forty meters and a pipe: a home on forty square meters of land and a connection to all the utilities of modernity.

A mutually agreed time tax had been enacted, such that a portion of the income and toil of those who had recently arrived on the island would go to those who had been there for decades, and this time tax was tapered in both directions, becoming a smaller and smaller sliver as one continued to reside, and then a larger and larger subsidy thereafter. Disruptions were enormous, and conflict did not vanish overnight, it persisted and simmered, but reports of its persistence and simmering seemed less than apocalyptic, and while some migrants continued to cling to properties they did not own under the law, and some migrants and some nativists too continued to detonate bombs and carry out knifings and shootings, Saeed and Nadia had the sense that overall, for most people, in Britain at least, existence went on in tolerable safety.

Saeed and Nadia's worker camp was bounded by a perimeter fence. Inside this were large pavilions of a grayish fabric that looked like plastic, supported by metal trusses in such a way that each reared up, and was airy within, and was resistant to the wind and rain. The two of them occupied a small curtained-off space in one of these dormitories, the curtains suspended from cables that ran almost as high as Saeed could reach, above which was empty space, as though the lower part of the pavilion was an open-topped maze, or the operating rooms of a huge field hospital.

They ate modestly, meals composed of grains and vegetables and some dairy, and when they were lucky, juiced fruit or a little meat. They were slightly hungry, yes, but slept well because the labor was lengthy and rigorous. The first dwellings that the workers of their camp had built were almost ready to be occupied, and Saeed and Nadia were not too far down the list, and so by the end of autumn they could look forward to moving into a home of their own. Their blisters had given way to calluses, and the rain did not much bother them anymore.

One night as Nadia slept on their cot beside Saeed she had a dream, a dream of the girl from Mykonos, and she dreamt that she had returned to the house they had first arrived at in London and had gone upstairs and passed back through the door to the Greek isle, and when Nadia woke she was almost panting, and felt her body alive, or alarmed, regardless changed, for the dream had seemed so real, and after that she found herself thinking of Mykonos from time to time.

FOR HIS PART Saeed often had dreams of his father, whose death had been reported to Saeed by a cousin who had recently managed to escape from their city, and with whom Saeed had connected by social media, the cousin having settled near Buenos Aires. This cousin told Saeed that Saeed's father had passed away from pneumonia, a lingering infection he had fought for months, initially just a cold but then much worse, and in the absence of antibiotics he had succumbed, but he had not been alone, his siblings were with him, and he had been buried next to his wife, as he had wished.

Saeed did not know how to mourn, how to express his remorse, from so great a distance. So he redoubled his work, and took on extra shifts even when he barely had the strength, and the wait for Nadia and him to receive their dwelling did not shorten, but it likewise did not increase, for other husbands and wives and mothers and fathers and men and women were working extra shifts as well, and Saeed's additional efforts served to maintain his and Nadia's ranking on the list.

Nadia was deeply affected by the news of the old man's passing, more even than she had expected. She tried to speak to Saeed about his father, but she stumbled over what to say, and on his side Saeed was quiet, unforthcoming. She felt herself touched by guilt from time to time, although she was unsure what precisely was making her guilty. All she knew was that when the feeling came it was a relief for her to be away from Saeed, at work on their separate work sites, a relief unless she thought about it, thought about being relieved not to be with him, because when she thought about this the guilt was usually not too far behind.

Saeed did not ask Nadia to pray with him for his father, and she did not offer, but when he was gathering a circle of acquaintances to pray in the long evening shadow cast by their dormitory, she said she would like to join the circle, to sit with Saeed and the others, even if not engaged in supplication herself, and he smiled and said there was no need. And she had no answer to this. But she stayed anyway, next to Saeed on the naked earth that had been stripped of plants by hundreds of thousands of footsteps and rutted by the tires of ponderously heavy vehicles, feeling for the first time unwelcome. Or perhaps unengaged. Or perhaps both.

FOR MANY, adjustment to this new world was difficult indeed, but for some it was also unexpectedly pleasant.

On Prinsengracht in the center of Amsterdam an elderly man stepped out onto the balcony of his little flat, one of the dozens into which what had been a pair of centuries-old canal houses and former warehouses had been converted, these flats looking out into a courtyard that was as lush with foliage as a tropical jungle, wet with greenness, in this city of water, and moss grew on the wooden edges of his balcony, and ferns also, and tendrils climbed up its sides, and there he had two chairs, two chairs from ages ago when there were two people living in his flat, though now there was one, his last lover having left him bitterly, and he sat down on one of these chairs and delicately rolled himself a cigarette, his fingers trembling, the paper crisp but with a hint of softness, from the damp, and the tobacco smell reminded him as it always did of his departed father, who would listen with him on his record player to audio recordings of science fiction adventures, and would pack and puff on his pipe, as sea creatures attacked a great submarine, the sounds of the wind and waves in the recording mixing with the sounds of the rain on their window, and the elderly man who was then a boy had thought, when I grow up I too will smoke, and here he was, a smoker for the better part of a century, about to light a cigarette, when he saw emerging from the common shed in the courtyard, where garden tools and the like were stored, and from which a steady stream of foreigners now came and went, a wrinkled man with a squint and a cane and a Panama hat, dressed as though for the tropics.

The elderly man looked at this wrinkled man and did not speak. He merely lit his cigarette and took a puff. The wrinkled man did not speak either: he walked slowly around the courtyard, leaning into his cane, which made scraping noises in the gravel of the footpath. Then the wrinkled man moved to reenter the shed, but before he left he turned to the elderly man, who was looking at him with a degree of disdain, and elegantly doffed his hat.

The elderly man was taken aback by this gesture, and sat still, as if transfixed, and before he could think of how to respond the wrinkled man stepped forward and was gone.

The next day the scene repeated itself. The elderly man was sitting on his balcony. The wrinkled man returned. They gazed upon each other. And this time when the wrinkled man doffed his hat, the elderly man raised a glass to him, a glass of fortified wine, which he happened to be drinking, and he did so with a serious but well-mannered nod of his head. Neither man smiled.

On the third day the elderly man asked the wrinkled man if he would care to join him on his balcony, and though the elderly man could not speak Brazilian Portuguese and the wrinkled man could not speak Dutch, they cobbled together a conversation, a conversation with many long gaps, but these gaps were eminently comfortable, almost unnoticed by the two men, as two ancient trees would not notice a few minutes or hours that passed without a breeze.

On his next visit the wrinkled man invited the elderly man to come with him through the black door that was inside the shed.

The elderly man did so, walking slowly, as the wrinkled man did as well, and at the other side of that door the elderly man found himself being helped to his feet by the wrinkled man in the hilly neighborhood of Santa Teresa, in Rio de Janeiro, on a day that was noticeably younger and warmer than the day he had left in Amsterdam. There the wrinkled man escorted him over tram tracks to the studio where he worked, and showed him some of his paintings, and the elderly man was too caught up in what was happening to be objective, but he thought these paintings were marked by real talent. He asked if he might buy one, and was instead given his choice as a gift.

A week later a war photographer who lived in a Prinsengracht flat that overlooked the same courtyard was the first neighbor to note the presence of this aged couple on the balcony opposite and below her. She was also, not long after, and to her considerable surprise, a witness to their very first kiss, which she captured, without expecting to, through the lens of her camera, and then deleted, later that night, in a gesture of uncharacteristic sentimentality and respect.

SOMETIMES SOMEONE from the press would descend on Saeed and Nadia's camp or work site, but more often denizens would themselves document and post and comment online upon what was going on. As usual, disasters attracted the most outside interest, such as a nativist raid that disabled machinery or destroyed dwelling units nearing completion or resulted in the severe beating of some workers who had strayed too far from camp. Or alternatively the knifing of a native foreman by a migrant or a fight among rival groups of migrants. But mostly there was little to report, just the day-to-day goings-on of countless people working and living and aging and falling in and out of love, as is the case everywhere, and so not deemed worthy of headline billing or thought to be of much interest to anyone but those directly involved.

No natives lived in the dormitories, for obvious reasons. But natives did labor alongside migrants on the work sites, usually as supervisors or as operators of heavy machinery, giant vehicles that resembled mechanized dinosaurs and would lift vast amounts of earth or roll flat hot strips of paving or churn concrete with the slow serenity of a masticating cow. Saeed had of course seen construction equipment before, but some of what he saw now dwarfed in scale anything he had previously seen, and in any case to work alongside a heaving and snorting building engine is not the same as glimpsing one from a distance, just as for an infantryman it is a markedly different experience to run alongside a tank in battle than it is for a child to watch one on parade.

Saeed worked on a road crew. His foreman was a knowl-
edgeable and experienced native with a few short tufts of white
hair ringing a mostly bald scalp that was covered by his helmet
unless he was wiping away his sweat at the end of the day. This
foreman was fair and strong and had a stark, afflicted counte-
nance. He did not make small talk but unlike many of the natives
he ate his lunch among the migrants who labored under him,
and he seemed to like Saeed, or if like was too strong a word, he
seemed at least to value Saeed's dedication, and often he sat next
to Saeed as he ate. Saeed also had the added advantage of being
among those workers who spoke English and so occupied a status midway between the foreman and the others on the team.

The team was a very large one, there being a surfeit of able
bodies and a shortage of machinery, and the foreman was constantly devising methods of using so many people efficiently. In
some ways he felt he was caught between the past and the future,
the past because when he had first started his career the balance
of tasks had similarly tipped more towards manual labor, and
the future because when he looked around him now at the almost unimaginable scale of what they were undertaking he felt
they were remodeling the Earth itself.

Saeed admired his foreman, the foreman having that sort of
quiet charisma that young men often gravitate towards, part of
which lay in the native man's not seeming the least interested in

being admired. Also, for Saeed and for many others on the team, their contact with the foreman was the closest and most extended of their contacts with any native, and so they looked at him as though he was the key to understanding their new home, its people and manners and ways and habits, which in a sense he was, though of course their very presence here meant that its people and manners and ways and habits were undergoing considerable change.

One time, as evening approached and the work for the day wound down, Saeed went up to his foreman and thanked him for all he was doing for the migrants. The foreman did not say anything. In that instant Saeed was reminded of those soldiers he had seen in the city of his birth, returning on leave from battle, who, when you pestered them for stories about where they had been and what they had done, looked at you as if you had no idea how much you were asking.

SAEED WOKE BEFORE DAWN the next day, his body tight and stiff. He tried not to move, out of consideration for Nadia, but opened his eyes and realized she was awake. His first instinct was to pretend he was still sleeping—he was exhausted, after all, and could have used more time undisturbed in bed— but the thought of her lying there and feeling alone was not a pleasant one, and besides she might have noticed the subterfuge. So he turned to her and asked, in a whisper, "Do you want to go outside?"

She nodded without gazing at him, and each of them rose and sat with their back to the other, on opposite sides of the cot, and fumbled in the dimness with their feet for their work boots. Laces rasped as they were cinched and tied. They could hear breathing and coughing and a child crying and the struggling sound of quiet sex. The pavilion's muted night-lighting was about the intensity of a crescent moon: enough to allow sleep, but also enough to see shapes, though not colors.

They made their way outside. The sky had begun to change, and was less dark now than indigo, and there were others scattered around, other couples and groups, but mostly solitary figures, unable to sleep, or at least unable to sleep any longer. It was cool but not cold, and Nadia and Saeed stood side by side and did not hold hands but felt the gentle pressure of their arms together, through their sleeves.

"I'm so tired, this morning," Nadia said.

"I know," said Saeed. "So am I."

Nadia wanted to say more to Saeed than that, but just then her throat felt raw, almost painful, and what else she would have liked to say was unable to find a way through to her tongue and her lips.

Saeed also had things on his mind. He knew he could have spoken to Nadia now. He knew he should have spoken to Nadia now, for they had time and were together and were not distracted. But he likewise could not bring himself to speak.

And so they walked instead, Saeed taking the first step, and Nadia following, and then both striding abreast each other, at a good clip, so that those who saw them saw what looked like a brace of workers marching, and not a couple out on a stroll. The camp was desolate at this hour, but there were birds out and about, a great many birds, flying or perched upon the pavilions and the perimeter fence, and Nadia and Saeed looked at these birds who had lost or would soon lose their trees to construction, and Saeed sometimes called out to them with a faint, sibilant, unpuckered whistle, like a balloon slowly deflating.

Nadia watched to see if any bird noticed his call, and did not on their walk see even one.

NADIA WORKED on a mostly female crew that laid pipe, colossal spools and pallets of it in different colors, orange and yellow and black and green. Through these pipes soon would run the lifeblood and thoughts of the new city, all those things that connect people without requiring them to move. Ahead of the pipe-layers was a digging machine, like a wolf spider or praying mantis, with a wide stance but a pair of dangerous-looking appendages at its front, coming together in a crenellated scraper near where its mouth would have been. This digging machine carved the trenches in the earth into which the pipe-layers would unfurl and unstack and lower and connect the pipes.

The driver of the digging machine was a portly native man with a non-native wife, a woman who looked native to Nadia but had apparently arrived from a nearby country two decades ago, and who quite possibly had retained a trace of her ancestral accent, but then again the natives had so many different accents that it was impossible for Nadia to say. This woman worked nearby as a supervisor in one of the food preparation units, and she would come to Nadia's work site on her lunch break when her husband was there, which was not always, because he dug trenches for multiple pipe-laying crews, and then the woman and her husband would unwrap sandwiches and unscrew thermoses and eat and chat and laugh.

As time passed, Nadia and some of the other women on her crew began to join them, for they were welcoming of company. The driver revealed himself to be a chatterbox and jokester, and relished the attention, and his wife seemed to relish it equally, though she spoke less, but she appeared to enjoy all these women listening enrapt to her husband. Perhaps this made him grow in stature in her own eyes. Nadia, who watched and smiled and usually said little in these gatherings, thought the couple a bit like the queen and king of a domain populated otherwise solely by women, a transient domain that would last only a few short seasons, and she wondered if perhaps they thought the same and had decided, nonetheless, to savor it.

IT WAS SAID that with every month there were more worker camps around London, but even if this were true Saeed and Nadia noticed an almost daily swelling of their own camp with new arrivals. Some came on foot, others in buses or vans. On their days off workers were encouraged to help out around the camp, and Saeed often volunteered to help process and settle the camp's latest additions.

Once he handled a small family, a mother, father, and daughter, three people whose skin was so fair that it seemed they had never seen the sun. He was struck by their eyelashes, which held the light improbably, and by their hands and cheeks, in which networks of tiny veins could be seen. He wondered where they came from, but he did not speak their language and they did not speak English, and he did not want to pry.

The mother was tall and narrow-shouldered, as tall as the father, and the daughter was a slightly smaller version of her mother, nearly equal to Saeed in height, though he suspected she was still very young, likely just thirteen or fourteen. They watched him with suspicion and in desperation, and Saeed was careful to speak softly and move slowly, as one does when meeting a nervous horse or puppy for the first time.

During the course of the afternoon he spent with them, Saeed only rarely heard them speak to one another in what he thought of as their odd language. Mostly they communicated by gesture, or with their eyes. Maybe, Saeed thought initially, they feared he might be able to understand them. Later he suspected something else. That they were ashamed, and that they did not yet know that shame, for the displaced, was a common feeling, and that there was, therefore, no particular shame in being ashamed.

He took them to their designated space in one of the new pavilions, unoccupied and basic, with a cot, and some fabric shelving hanging from one of the cables, and he left them there to settle in, left the three of them staring and motionless. But when he returned an hour later to bring them to the mess tent for lunch, and called out, and the mother pushed aside the flap that served as their front door, and he glimpsed inside, what he glimpsed was a home, with the shelves all full, and neat bundles of belongings on the ground, and a throw on the cot, and also on the cot the daughter, her back unsupported but erect, her legs crossed at the shins, so that her thighs rested on her feet, and in her lap a little notebook or diary, in which she was writing furiously until the last moment, until the mother called out her name, and which she then locked, with a key that she wore on a string around her neck, and placed in one of the piles of belongings that must have been hers, thrust the diary into the middle of the pile so that it was hidden.

She fell in behind her parents, who nodded at Saeed in recognition, and he turned and led them all from that place, a place that was already beginning to be theirs, to another where going forward they could reliably find a meal.

THE NORTHERN SUMMER EVENINGS were endless. Saeed and Nadia often fell asleep before it was fully dark, and before they fell asleep they often sat outside on the ground with their backs to the dormitory, on their phones, wandering far and wide but not together, even though they appeared to be together, and sometimes he or she would look up and feel on their face the wind blowing through the shattered fields all about them.

They put their lack of conversation down to exhaustion, for by the end of the day they were usually so tired they could barely speak, and phones themselves have the innate power of distancing one from one's physical surroundings, which accounted for part of it, but Saeed and Nadia no longer touched each other when they lay in bed, not in that way, and not because their curtained-off space in the pavilion seemed less than entirely private, or not only because of that, and when they did speak at length, they, a pair once not used to arguing, tended to argue, as though their nerves were so raw that extended encounters evoked a sensation of pain.

Every time a couple moves they begin, if their attention is still drawn to one another, to see each other differently, for personalities are not a single immutable color, like white or blue, but rather illuminated screens, and the shades we reflect depend much on what is around us. So it was with Saeed and Nadia, who found themselves changed in each other's eyes in this new place.

To Nadia, Saeed was if anything more handsome than he had been before, his hard work and his gauntness suiting him, giving him a contemplative air, making out of his boyishness a man of substance. She noticed other women looking at him from time to time, and yet she herself felt strangely unmoved by his handsomeness, as though he were a rock or a house, something she might admire but without any real desire.

He had two or three white hairs in the stubble of his beard now, new arrivals this summer, and he prayed more regularly, every morning and evening, and perhaps on his lunch breaks too. When he spoke he spoke of paving and positions on waiting lists and politics, but not of his parents, and not anymore of travel, of all the places they might one day see together, or of the stars.

He was drawn to people from their country, both in the labor camp and online. It seemed to Nadia that the farther they moved from the city of their birth, through space and through time, the more he sought to strengthen his connection to it, tying ropes to the air of an era that for her was unambiguously gone.

To Saeed, Nadia looked much the same as she did when they first met, which is to say strikingly fetching, if vastly more tired. But it was inexplicable that she continued to wear her black robes, and it grated on him a bit, for she did not pray, and she avoided speaking their language, and she avoided their people, and sometimes he wanted to shout, well take it off then, and then he would wince inwardly, since he believed he loved her, and his resentment, when it bubbled up like this, made him angry with himself, with the man he seemed to be becoming, a less than romantic man, which was not the sort of man he believed a man should aspire to be.

Saeed wanted to feel for Nadia what he had always felt for Nadia, and the potential loss of this feeling left him unmoored, adrift in a world where one could go anywhere but still find nothing. He was certain that he cared for her and wished good for her and wanted to protect her. She was the entirety of his close family now, and he valued family above all, and when the warmth between them seemed lacking his sorrow was immense, so immense that he was uncertain whether all his losses had not combined into a core of loss, and in this core, this center, the death of his mother and the death of his father and the possible death of his ideal self who had loved his woman so well were like a single death that only hard work and prayer might allow him to withstand.

Saeed made it a point to smile with Nadia, at least sometimes, and he hoped she would feel something warm and caring when he smiled, but what she felt was sorrow and the sense that they were better than this, and that together they had to find a way out.

AND SO WHEN SHE SUGGESTED one day, out of the blue, under the drone-crossed sky and in the invisible network of surveillance that radiated out from their phones, recording and capturing and logging everything, that they abandon this place, and give up their position on the housing list, and all they had built here, and pass through a nearby door she had heard of, to the new city of Marin, on the Pacific Ocean, close to San Francisco, he did not argue, or even resist, as she thought he might, and instead he said yes, and both of them were filled with hope, hope that they would be able to rekindle their relationship, to reconnect with their relationship, as it had been not long ago, and to elude, through a distance spanning a third of the globe, what it seemed in danger of becoming.

TEN

I N MARIN, the higher up the hills one went, the fewer services there were, but the better the scenery. Nadia and Saeed were relative latecomers to this new city, and the lower slopes were all taken, and so they found a spot high up, with a view across and through the Golden Gate Bridge of San Francisco and the bay, when it was clear, and a view of scattered islands floating on a sea of clouds, when the fog rolled in.

They assembled a shanty with a corrugated metal roof and discarded packing crate sides. This, as their neighbors had explained, was earthquake friendly: it might fall in a tremor, but it was unlikely to do its occupants too much harm because of its relatively light weight. Wireless data signals were strong, and they secured a solar panel and battery set with a universal outlet, which accepted plugs from all around the world, and a rainwater collector fashioned from synthetic fabric and a bucket, and dew collectors that fit inside plastic bottles like the filaments of upside-down lightbulbs, and so life, while basic, was not quite as rough, nor as cut off, as otherwise it might have been.

From their shanty the fog was a living thing: moving, thickening, slipping, thinning out. It revealed the invisible, what was happening in the water and in the air, for suddenly heat and cold and damp could not merely be felt on one's skin but be seen through their atmospheric effects. It seemed to Nadia and Saeed that somehow they lived at once on the ocean and among the peaks.

For work Nadia hiked down, first through other unpiped and unwired districts like their own, then through those where grid electricity had been installed, and then through those where roads and running water had reached, and from there she caught a ride on a bus or pickup truck to her place of employment, a food cooperative in a hastily built commercial zone outside Sausalito.

Marin was overwhelmingly poor, all the more so in comparison to the sparkling affluence of San Francisco. But there was nonetheless a spirit of at least intermittent optimism that refused entirely to die in Marin, perhaps because Marin was less violent than most of the places its residents had fled, or because of the view, its position on the edge of a continent, overlooking the world's widest ocean, or because of the mix of its people, or its proximity to that realm of giddy technology that stretched down the bay like a bent thumb, ever poised to meet the curved finger of Marin in a slightly squashed gesture that all would be okay.

ONE NIGHT Nadia brought back some weed a coworker had given her. She did not know how Saeed would react, and this fact struck her as she hiked home. In the city of their birth they had smoked joints together with pleasure, but a year had passed since then, and he had changed since then, and perhaps she had changed too, and the distance that had opened between them was such that things once taken for granted could be taken for granted no longer.

Saeed was more melancholic than he had been before, understandably, and also more quiet and devout. She sometimes felt that his praying was not neutral towards her, in fact she suspected it carried a hint of reproach, though why she felt this she could not say, for he had never told her to pray nor berated her for not praying. But in his devotions was ever more devotion, and towards her it seemed there was ever less.

She had considered rolling a joint outdoors and smoking the weed by herself, without Saeed, concealed from Saeed, and it had surprised her to be considering this, and made her wonder about the ways in which she was herself putting barriers between her and him. She did not know if these gaps that had been widening were mostly her doing or his, but she knew she still harbored tenderness for him, and so she had brought the weed home, and it was only when she sat beside him on the car seat they had bartered for and used now as a sofa, that she realized, from her nervousness, that how in this moment he responded to the weed was a matter of portentous significance to her.

Her leg and arm touched Saeed's leg and arm, and he was warm through his clothing, and he sat in a way that suggested exhaustion. But he also managed a tired smile, which was encouraging, and when she opened her fist to reveal what was inside, as she had once before done on her rooftop a brief lifetime ago, and he saw the weed, he started to laugh, almost soundlessly, a gentle rumble, and he said, his voice uncoiling like a slow, languid exhalation of marijuana-scented smoke, "Fantastic."

Saeed rolled the joint for them both, Nadia barely containing her jubilation, and wanting to hug him but restraining herself. He lit it and they consumed it, lungs burning, and the first thing that struck her was that this weed was much stronger than the hash back home, and she was quite floored by its effects, and also well on her way to becoming a little paranoid, and finding it difficult to speak.

For a while they sat in silence, the temperature dropping outside. Saeed fetched a blanket and they bundled it around themselves. And then, not looking at each other, they started to
laugh, and Nadia laughed until she cried.

IN MARIN THERE WERE almost no natives, these people
having died out or been exterminated long ago, and one would
see them only occasionally, at impromptu trading posts—or
perhaps more often, but wrapped in clothes and guises and be-
haviors indistinguishable from anyone else. At the trading posts
they would sell beautiful silver jewelry and soft leather gar-
ments and colorful textiles, and the elders among them seemed
not infrequently to be possessed of a limitless patience that was
matched by a limitless sorrow. Tales were told at these places
that people from all over now gathered to hear, for the tales of
these natives felt appropriate to this time of migration, and gave
listeners much-needed sustenance.

And yet it was not quite true to say there were almost no
natives, nativeness being a relative matter, and many others considered themselves native to this country, by which they meant
that they or their parents or their grandparents or the grandparents of their grandparents had been born on the strip of land that
stretched from the mid-northern-Pacific to the mid-northern-

Atlantic, that their existence here did not owe anything to a physical migration that had occurred in their lifetimes. It seemed to Saeed that the people who advocated this position most strongly, who claimed the rights of nativeness most forcefully, tended to be drawn from the ranks of those with light skin who looked most like the natives of Britain—and as had been the case with many of the natives of Britain, many of these people too seemed stunned by what was happening to their homeland, what had already happened in so brief a period, and some seemed angry as well.

A third layer of nativeness was composed of those who others thought directly descended, even in the tiniest fraction of their genes, from the human beings who had been brought from Africa to this continent centuries ago as slaves. While this layer of nativeness was not vast in proportion to the rest, it had vast importance, for society had been shaped in reaction to it, and unspeakable violence had occurred in relation to it, and yet it endured, fertile, a stratum of soil that perhaps made possible all future transplanted soils, and to which Saeed in particular was attracted, since at a place of worship where he had gone one Friday the communal prayer was led by a man who came from this tradition and spoke of this tradition, and Saeed had found, in the weeks he and Nadia had been in Marin, this man's words to be full of soul-soothing wisdom.

The preacher was a widower, and his wife had come from the same country as Saeed, and so the preacher knew some of Saeed's language, and his approach to religion was partly familiar to Saeed, while at the same time partly novel, too. The preacher did not solely preach. Mainly he worked to feed and shelter his congregants, and teach them English. He ran a small but efficient organization staffed with volunteers, young men and women, all Saeed's color or darker, which Saeed too had soon joined, and among these young men and women that Saeed now labored alongside was one woman in particular, the preacher's daughter, with curly hair she wore tied up high on her head with a cloth, this one woman the one woman in particular that Saeed avoided speaking to, because whenever he looked at her he felt his breath tighten within him, and he thought guiltily of Nadia, and he thought further that here, for him, lay something best not explored at all.

NADIA PERCEIVED the presence of this woman not in the form of a distancing by Saeed, as might have been expected, but rather as a warming up and reaching out. Saeed seemed happier, and keen to smoke joints with Nadia at the end of the day, or at least share a couple of puffs, for they had adjusted their consumption in recognition of the local weed's potency, and they began to speak of nothings once again, of travel and the stars and the clouds and the music they heard all around them from the other shanties. She felt bits of the old Saeed returning.

She wished, therefore, that she could be the old Nadia. But much as she enjoyed their chats and the improved mood between them, they rarely touched, and her desire to be touched by him, long subsided, did not flicker back into flame. It seemed to Nadia that something had gone quiet inside her. She spoke to him, but her words were muffled to her own ears. She lay beside Saeed, falling asleep, but not craving his hands or his mouth on her body—stifled, as if Saeed were becoming her brother, though never having had a brother she was unsure what that term meant.

It was not that her sensuality, her sense of the erotic, had died. She found herself aroused readily, by a beautiful man she passed as she walked down to work, by memories of the musician who had been her first lover, by thoughts of the girl from Mykonos. And sometimes when Saeed was out or asleep she pleasured herself, and when she pleasured herself she thought increasingly of that girl, the girl from Mykonos, and the strength of her response no longer surprised her.

WHEN SAEED WAS a child he had first prayed out of curiosity. He had seen his mother and father praying, and the act held

a certain mystery for him. His mother used to pray in her bedroom, perhaps once a day, unless it was a particularly holy time,
or there had been a death in the family, or an illness, in which
case she prayed more often. His father prayed mainly on Fri-
days, under normal circumstances, and only sporadically during
the week. Saeed would see them preparing to pray, and see them
praying, and see their faces after they had prayed, usually smiling, as though relieved, or released, or comforted, and he would
wonder what happened when one prayed, and he was curious to
experience it for himself, and so he asked to learn before his parents had yet thought of teaching him, and his mother provided
the requisite instruction one particularly hot summer, and that is
how, for him, it began. Until the end of his days, prayer sometimes reminded Saeed of his mother, and his parents' bedroom
with its slight smell of perfume, and the ceiling fan churning in
the heat.

As he was entering his teens, Saeed's father asked Saeed if he
would like to accompany him to the weekly communal prayer.
Saeed said yes, and thereafter every Friday, without fail, Saeed's
father would drive home and collect his son and Saeed would
pray with his father and the men, and prayer for him became
about being a man, being one of the men, a ritual that connected
him to adulthood and to the notion of being a particular sort of
man, a gentleman, a gentle man, a man who stood for commu-

nity and faith and kindness and decency, a man, in other words, like his father. Young men pray for different things, of course, but some young men pray to honor the goodness of the men who raised them, and Saeed was very much a young man of this mold.

By the time he entered university, Saeed's parents prayed more often than they had when he was younger, maybe because they had lost a great many loved ones by that age, or maybe because the transient natures of their own lives were gradually becoming less hidden from them, or maybe because they worried for their son in a country that seemed to worship money above all, no matter how much other forms of worship were given lip service, or maybe simply because their personal relationships with prayer had deepened and become more meaningful over the years. Saeed too prayed more often in this period, at the very least once a day, and he valued the discipline of it, the fact that it was a code, a promise he had made, and that he stood by.

Now, though, in Marin, Saeed prayed even more, several times a day, and he prayed fundamentally as a gesture of love for what had gone and would go and could be loved in no other way. When he prayed he touched his parents, who could not otherwise be touched, and he touched a feeling that we are all children who lose our parents, all of us, every man and woman and boy and girl, and we too will all be lost by those who come after us and love us, and this loss unites humanity, unites every human being, the temporary nature of our being-ness, and our shared sorrow, the heartache we each carry and yet too often refuse to acknowledge in one another, and out of this Saeed felt it might be possible, in the face of death, to believe in humanity's potential for building a better world, and so he prayed as a lament, as a consolation, and as a hope, but he felt that he could not express this to Nadia, that he did not know how to express this to Nadia, this mystery that prayer linked him to, and it was so important to express it, and somehow he was able to express it to the preacher's daughter, the first time they had a proper conversation, at a small ceremony he happened upon after work, which turned out to be a remembrance for her mother, who had been from Saeed's country, and was prayed for communally on each anniversary of her death, and her daughter, who was also the preacher's daughter, said to Saeed, who was standing near her, so tell me about my mother's country, and when Saeed spoke he did not mean to but he spoke of his own mother, and he spoke for a long time, and the preacher's daughter spoke for a long time, and when they finished speaking it was already late at night.

SAEED AND NADIA WERE LOYAL, and whatever name they gave their bond they each in their own way believed it required them to protect the other, and so neither talked much of drifting apart, not wanting to inflict a fear of abandonment, while also themselves quietly feeling that fear, the fear of the severing of their tie, the end of the world they had built together, a world of shared experiences in which no one else would share, and a shared intimate language that was unique to them, and a sense that what they might break was special and likely irreplaceable. But while fear was part of what kept them together for those first few months in Marin, more powerful than fear was the desire that each see the other find firmer footing before they let go, and thus in the end their relationship did in some senses come to resemble that of siblings, in that friendship was its strongest element, and unlike many passions, theirs managed to cool slowly, without curdling into its reverse, anger, except intermittently. Of this, in later years, both were glad, and both would also wonder if this meant that they had made a mistake, that if they had but waited and watched their relationship would have flowered again, and so their memories took on potential, which is of course how our greatest nostalgias are born.

Jealousy did rear itself in their shanty from time to time, and the couple that was uncoupling did argue, but mostly they granted each other more space, a process that had been ongoing for quite a while, and if there was sorrow and alarm in this, there was relief too, and the relief was stronger.

There was also closeness, for the end of a couple is like a death, and the notion of death, of temporariness, can remind us of the value of things, which it did for Saeed and Nadia, and so even though they spoke less and did less together, they saw each other more, although not more often.

One night one of the tiny drones that kept a watch on their district, part of a swarm, and not larger than a hummingbird, crashed into the transparent plastic flap that served as both door and window of their shanty, and Saeed gathered its motionless iridescent body and showed it to Nadia, and she smiled and said they ought to give it a burial, and they dug a small hole right there, in the hilly soil where it had fallen, using a spade, and then covered this grave again, pressed it flat, and Nadia asked if Saeed was planning on offering a prayer for the departed automaton, and he laughed and said maybe he would.

SOMETIMES THEY LIKED to sit outside their shanty in the open air, where they could hear all the sounds of the new settlement, sounds like a festival, music and voices and a motorcycle and the wind, and they wondered what Marin had been like before. People said it had been beautiful, but in a different way, and empty.

The winter that year was a season that had splashes of au-

tumn and spring mixed up in it, even an occasional day of summer. Once as they sat it was so warm that they did not need
sweaters, and they watched as the sunlight poured down in an-
gled bursts through gaps in the bright, roiling clouds, and lit
up bits of San Francisco and Oakland and the otherwise dark
waters of the bay.

"What's that?" Nadia asked Saeed, pointing to a flat and
geometric shape.

"They call it Treasure Island," Saeed said.

She smiled. "What an interesting name."

"Yes."

"The one behind it should be called Treasure Island. It's
more mysterious."

Saeed nodded. "And that bridge, Treasure Bridge."

Someone was cooking over an open fire nearby, beyond the
next ridge of shanties. They could see a thin trail of smoke and
smell something. Not meat. Sweet potatoes maybe. Or maybe
plantains.

Saeed hesitated, then took Nadia's hand, his palm covering
her knuckles. She curved her fingers, furling the tips of his
around hers. She thought she felt his pulse. They sat like that for
a long while.

"I'm hungry," she said.

"So am I."

She almost kissed him on his prickly cheek. "Well, some-where down there is everything in the world anyone could want to eat."

NOT FAR TO THE SOUTH, in the town of Palo Alto, lived an old woman who had lived in the same house her entire life. Her parents had brought her to this house when she was born, and her mother had passed on there when she was a teenager, and her father when she was in her twenties, and her husband had joined her there, and her two children had grown up in this house, and she had lived alone with them when she divorced, and later with her second husband, their stepfather, and her children had moved off to college and not returned, and her second husband had died two years ago, and throughout this time she had never moved, traveled, yes, but never moved, and yet it seemed the world had moved, and she barely recognized the town that existed outside her property.

The old woman had become a rich woman on paper, the house now worth a fortune, and her children were always pestering her to sell it, saying she didn't need all that space. But she told them to be patient, it would be theirs when she died, which wouldn't be long now, and she said this kindly, to sharpen the bite of it, and to remind them how much they were motivated by money, money they spent without having, which she had never done, always saving for a rainy day, even if only a little.

One of her granddaughters went to the great university nearby, a university that had gone from being a local secret to among the world's most famous in the space of the old woman's lifetime. This granddaughter came to see her, often as much as once a week. She was the only one of the old woman's descendants who did this, and the old woman adored her, and also sometimes felt baffled by her: looking at her granddaughter she thought she saw what she would have looked like had she been born in China, for the granddaughter had features of the old woman, and yet looked to the old woman, overall, more or less, but mostly more, Chinese.

There was a rise that led up to the old woman's street, and when she was a little girl the old woman used to push her bike up and then get on and zoom back down without pedaling, bikes being heavy in those days and hard to take uphill, especially when you were small, as she was then, and your bike too big, as hers had been. She had liked to see how far she could glide without stopping, flashing through the intersections, ready to brake, but not overly ready, because there had been a lot less traffic, at least as far as she could remember.

She had always had carp in a mossy pond in the back of her house, carp that her granddaughter called goldfish, and she had known the names of almost everyone on her street, and most had been there a long time, they were old California, from families that were California families, but over the years they had changed more and more rapidly, and now she knew none of them, and saw no reason to make the effort, for people bought and sold houses the way they bought and sold stocks, and every year someone was moving out and someone was moving in, and now all these doors from who knows where were opening, and all sorts of strange people were around, people who looked more at home than she was, even the homeless ones who spoke no English, more at home maybe because they were younger, and when she went out it seemed to her that she too had migrated, that everyone migrates, even if we stay in the same houses our whole lives, because we can't help it.

We are all migrants through time.

ELEVEN

ALL OVER THE WORLD people were slipping away from where they had been, from once fertile plains cracking with dryness, from seaside villages gasping beneath tidal surges, from overcrowded cities and murderous battlefields, and slipping away from other people too, people they had in some cases loved, as Nadia was slipping away from Saeed, and Saeed from Nadia.

It was Nadia who first brought up the topic of her moving out of the shanty, said in passing as she sipped on a joint, taking the slenderest of puffs, held in her lungs even as the idea of what she had said scented the air. Saeed did not say anything in response, he merely took a hit himself, contained it tightly, exhaling later into her exhale. In the morning when she woke he was looking at her, and he stroked the hair from her face, as he had not done for months, and he said if anyone should leave the home they had built it was him. But as he said this he felt he was acting, or if not acting then so confused as to be incapable of gauging his own sincerity. He did think that he ought to be the one to go, that he had reparations to make for becoming close to the preacher's daughter. So it was not his words that felt to him like an act, but rather his stroking of Nadia's hair, which, it seemed to him in that moment, he might never have permission to stroke again. Nadia too felt both comforted and discomforted by this physical intimacy, and she said that no, she wanted to be the one to leave if one of them left, and she likewise detected an untruth in her words, for she knew the matter was one not of if, but of when, and that when would be soon.

A spoilage had begun to manifest itself in their relationship, and each recognized it would be better to part now, ere worse came, but days passed before they discussed it again, and as they discussed it Nadia was already packing her things into a back-pack and a satchel, and so their discussion of her departure was not, as it pretended to be, a discussion of her departure, but a navigation, through words that said otherwise, of their fear of what would come next, and when Saeed insisted he would carry her bags for her, she insisted he not do so, and they did not embrace or kiss then, they stood facing each other at the threshold of the shanty that had been theirs, and they did not shake hands either, they looked each at the other, for a long, long time, any gesture seeming inadequate, and in silence Nadia turned and walked away into the misty drizzle, and her raw face was wet and alive.

AT THE FOOD COOPERATIVE where Nadia worked there were rooms available, storerooms upstairs, in the back. These rooms had cots, and workers in good standing at the cooperative could use them, stay there, seemingly indefinitely, provided one's colleagues thought the need to stay was valid, and one put in enough extra hours to cover the occupancy, and while this practice was likely in violation of some code or other, regulations were not much in force anymore, even here near Sausalito.

Nadia knew people stayed at the cooperative, but she did not know how the policy worked, and no one had told her. For although she was a woman, and the cooperative was run and staffed predominantly by women, her black robe was thought by many to be off-putting, or self-segregating, or in any case vaguely menacing, and so few of her colleagues had really reached out to her until the day that a pale-skinned tattooed man had come in while she was working the till and had placed a pistol on the counter and said to her, "So what the fuck do you think of that?"

Nadia did not know what to say and so she said nothing, not challenging his gaze but not looking away either. Her eyes focused on a spot around his chin, and they stood like this, in silence, for a moment, and the man repeated himself, a bit less steadily the second time, and then, without robbing the cooperative, or shooting Nadia, he left, taking his gun and cursing and kicking over a bushel of lumpy apples as he went.

Whether it was because they were impressed by her mettle in the face of danger or because they recalibrated their sense of who was threat and who was threatened or because they now simply had something to talk about, several people on her shifts began chatting with her a lot more after that. She felt she was beginning to belong, and when one told her about the option of living at the cooperative, and that she could avail herself of it if her family was oppressing her, or, another added quickly, even if she just felt like a change, the possibility struck Nadia with a shock of recognition, as though a door was opening up, a door in this case shaped like a room.

It was into this room that Nadia moved when she separated from Saeed. The room smelled of potatoes and thyme and mint and the cot smelled a little of people, even though it was reasonably clean, and there was no record player, and no scope to decorate either, the room continuing to be used as a storeroom. But Nadia was nonetheless reminded of her apartment in the city of her birth, which she had loved, reminded of what it was like to live there alone, and while the first night she slept not at all, and the second only fitfully, as the days passed she slept better and better, and this room came to feel to her like home.

The locality around Marin seemed to be rousing itself from a profound and collective low in those days. It has been said that depression is a failure to imagine a plausible desirable future for oneself, and, not just in Marin, but in the whole region, in the Bay Area, and in many other places too, places both near and far, the apocalypse appeared to have arrived and yet it was not apocalyptic, which is to say that while the changes were jarring they were not the end, and life went on, and people found things to do and ways to be and people to be with, and plausible desirable futures began to emerge, unimaginable previously, but not unimaginable now, and the result was something not unlike relief.

Indeed there was a great creative flowering in the region, especially in music. Some were calling this a new jazz age, and one could walk around Marin and see all kinds of ensembles, humans with humans, humans with electronics, dark skin with light skin with gleaming metal with matte plastic, computerized music and unamplified music and even people who wore masks or hid themselves from view. Different types of music gathered different tribes of people, tribes that had not existed before, as is always the case, and at one such gathering, Nadia saw the head cook from the cooperative, a handsome woman with strong arms, and this woman saw Nadia seeing her and nodded in recognition. Later they wound up standing beside one another and talking, not much, and just in between the songs, but when the set ended they did not leave, they continued to listen and talk during the set that followed.

The cook had eyes that seemed an almost inhuman blue, or rather a blue that Nadia had not previously thought of as human, so pale as to suggest, if you looked at them when the cook was looking away, that these eyes might be blind. But when they looked at you there was no doubt that they saw, for this woman gazed so powerfully, she was such a watcher, that her watching hit you like a physical force, and Nadia felt a thrill being seen by her, and seeing her in turn.

The cook was, of course, an expert in food, and over the coming weeks and months she introduced Nadia to all sorts of old cuisines, and to new cuisines that were being born, for many of the world's foods were coming together and being reformed in Marin, and the place was a taster's paradise, and the rationing that was under way meant you were always a little hungry, and therefore primed to savor what you got, and Nadia had never before delighted in tasting as she did in the company of the cook, who reminded her a bit of a cowboy, and who made love, when they made love, with a steady hand and a sure eye and a mouth that did little but did it so very well.

SAEED AND THE PREACHER'S DAUGHTER likewise drew close, and while there was some resistance by others to this, Saeed's ancestors not having undergone the experience of slavery and its aftermath on this continent, the effects of the preacher's particular brand of religion diminished this resistance, and with time camaraderie did too, the work Saeed did alongside his fellow volunteers, and then there was the fact that the preacher had married a woman from Saeed's country, and also that the preacher's daughter was born of a woman from Saeed's country, and so the pair's closeness, even if it prompted unease in some quarters, was tolerated, and for the pair themselves their closeness carried both a spark of the exotic and the comfort of familiarity, as many couplings do, when they first begin.

Saeed would seek her out in the mornings, when he arrived for work, and they would talk and smile sidelong, and she might touch his elbow, and they would sit together at the communal lunch, and in the evenings when their work was done for the day they would walk through Marin, hike up and down the paths and the streets that were forming, and once they walked past Saeed's shanty, and he told her it was his, and the next time they walked by she asked to see the inside of it, and they went in, and they shut the plastic flap behind them.

The preacher's daughter found in Saeed an attitude to faith that intrigued her, and she found the expansiveness of his gaze upon the universe, the way he spoke of the stars and of the people of the world, very sexy, and his touch as well, and she liked the cut of his face, how it reminded her of her mother and hence her childhood. And Saeed found her remarkably easy to talk to, not just because she listened well or spoke well, which she did, but because she prompted him to want to listen and speak, and he had from the outset found her so attractive that she was almost difficult to look at, and also, though he did not say this to her, or even care to think it, there were aspects of her that were much like Nadia.

The preacher's daughter was among the local campaign leaders of the plebiscite movement, which sought a ballot on the question of the creation of a regional assembly for the Bay Area, with members elected on the principle of one person one vote, regardless of where one came from. How this assembly would coexist with other preexisting bodies of government was as yet undecided. It might at first have only a moral authority, but that authority could be substantial, for unlike those other entities for which some humans were not human enough to exercise suffrage, this new assembly would speak from the will of all the people, and in the face of that will, it was hoped, greater justice might be less easily denied.

One day she showed Saeed a little device that looked to him like a thimble. She was so happy, and he asked her why, and she said that this could be the key to the plebiscite, that it made it possible to tell one person from another and ensure they could vote only once, and it was being manufactured in vast numbers, at a cost so small as to be almost nothing, and he held it on his palm and discovered to his surprise that it was no heavier than a feather.

WHEN NADIA WALKED AWAY from their shanty, she and Saeed did not communicate for the rest of the day, nor on the day that followed. It was the longest cessation of contact between them since they had left the city of their birth. On the evening of their second day apart Saeed called her to ask how she was doing, to inquire if she was safe, and also to hear her voice, and the voice he heard was familiar and strange, and as they spoke he wanted to see her, but he withstood this, and they hung up without arranging a meeting. She called him the following evening, again a brief call, and after that they messaged or spoke to one another on most days, and while their first weekend apart passed separately, on the second weekend they agreed to meet for a walk by the ocean, and they walked to the sound of the wind and the crashing waves and in the hiss of the spray.

They met again for a walk the weekend after that, and again the weekend after that, and there was a sadness to these meetings, for they missed each other, and they were lonely and somewhat adrift in this new place. Sometimes after they met Nadia would feel part of herself torn inside, and sometimes Saeed would feel this, and both teetered on the cusp of making some physical gesture that would bind them each to the other again, but both in the end managed to resist.

The ritual of their weekly walk was interrupted, as such connections are, by the strengthening of other pulls on their time, the pull of the cook on Nadia, of the preacher's daughter on Saeed, and of new acquaintances. While the first shared weekend walk that they skipped was noticed sharply by them both, the second was not so much, and the third almost not at all, and soon they were meeting only once a month or so, and several days would pass in between a message or a call.

They lingered in this state of tangential connection as winter gave way to spring—though seasons in Marin seemed sometimes to last only for a small portion of a day, to change in the time that one took off one's jacket or put on one's sweater—and they lingered still in this state as a warm spring gave way to a cool summer. Neither much enjoyed catching unexpected glimpses of their former lover's new existence online, and so they distanced themselves from each other on social networks, and while they wished to look out for each other, and to keep tabs on each other, staying in touch took a toll on them, serving as an unsettling reminder of a life not lived, and also they grew less worried each for the other, less worried that the other would need them to be happy, and eventually a month went by without any contact, and then a year, and then a lifetime.

OUTSIDE MARRAKESH, in the hills, overlooking the palatial home of a man who might once have been called a prince and a woman who might once have been called a foreigner, there was a maid in an emptying village who could not speak and, perhaps for this reason, could not imagine leaving. She worked in the great house below, a house that had fewer servants now than it did in the year before, and fewer then than in the year before that, its retainers having gradually fled, or moved, but not the maid, who rode to work each morning on a bus, and who survived by virtue of her salary.

The maid was not old, but her husband and daughter were gone, her husband not long after their marriage, to Europe, from which he had not returned, and from which he had eventually stopped sending money. The maid's mother had said it was because she could not speak and because she had given him a taste of the pleasures of the flesh, unknown to him before their marriage, and so she had armed him as a man and been disarmed by nature as a woman. But her mother had been hard, and the maid had not thought the trade a bad one, for her husband had given her a daughter, and this daughter had given her companionship on her journey through life, and though her daughter too had passed through the doors, she returned to visit, and each time she returned she told the maid to come with her, and the maid said no, for she had a sense of the fragility of things, and she felt she was a small plant in a small patch of soil held between the rocks of a dry and windy place, and she was not wanted by the world, and here she was at least known, and she was tolerated, and that was a blessing.

The maid was of an age at which men had stopped seeing her. She had had the body of a woman when she was still a girl, when she was married off, so young, and her body had ripened further after she birthed and nursed her child, and men had once paused to look at her, not at her face, but at her figure, and she had often been alarmed by those looks, in part because of the danger in them, and in part because she knew how they changed when she was revealed to be mute, and so the end of being seen was mostly a relief. Mostly, almost entirely, yet not entirely, for life had given the maid no space for the luxuries of vanity, but even so, she was human.

The maid did not know her age, but she knew she was younger than the mistress of the house where she worked, whose hair was still jet and whose posture was still erect and whose dresses were still cut with the intention to arouse. The mistress seemed not to have aged at all in the many years the maid had worked for her. From a distance she might be mistaken for a very young woman, while the maid seemed to have aged doubly, perhaps for them both, as if her occupation had been to age, to exchange the magic of months for bank notes and food.

In the summer that Saeed and Nadia were parting into separate lives, the maid's daughter came to see the maid in that village where almost everyone had gone and they drank coffee under the evening sky and looked out at the reddening dust rising in the south and daughter asked mother again to come with her.

The maid looked at her daughter, who looked to her as though she had captured the best of her, and of her husband too, for she could see him in her, and of her mother, whose voice came from her daughter's mouth, strong and low, but not her words, for her daughter's words were utterly unlike her mother's had been, they were quick and nimble and new. The maid placed her hand on her daughter's hand and brought it to her lips and kissed it, the skin of her lips clinging for an instant to the skin of her child, clinging even as she lowered her daughter's hand, the shape of lips being mutable in this way, and the maid smiled and shook her head.

One day she might go, she thought.

But not today.

TWELVE

HALF A CENTURY LATER Nadia returned for the first time to the city of her birth, where the fires she had witnessed in her youth had burned themselves out long ago, the lives of cities being far more persistent and more gently cyclical than those of people, and the city she found herself in was not a heaven but it was not a hell, and it was familiar but also unfamiliar, and as she wandered about slowly, exploring, she was informed of the proximity of Saeed, and after standing motionless for a considerable moment she communicated with him, and they agreed to meet.

They met at a café near her old building, which still stood, though most of the others close by had changed, and they sat beside one another on two adjacent sides of a small square table, under the sky, and they looked at each other, sympathetic looks, for time had done what time does, but looks of particular recognition, and they watched the young people of this city pass, young people who had no idea how bad things once were, except what they studied in history, which was perhaps as it should be, and they sipped their coffees, and they spoke.

Their conversation navigated two lives, with vital details highlighted and excluded, and it was also a dance, for they were former lovers, and they had not wounded each other so deeply as to have lost their ability to find a rhythm together, and they grew younger and more playful as the coffee in their cups diminished, and Nadia said imagine how different life would be if I had agreed to marry you, and Saeed said imagine how different it would be if I had agreed to have sex with you, and Nadia said we were having sex, and Saeed considered and smiled and said yes I suppose we were.

Above them bright satellites transited in the darkening sky and the last hawks were returning to the rest of their nests and around them passersby did not pause to look at this old woman in her black robe or this old man with his stubble.

They finished their coffees. Nadia asked if Saeed had been to the deserts of Chile and seen the stars and was it all he had imagined it would be. He nodded and said if she had an evening free he would take her, it was a sight worth seeing in this life, and she shut her eyes and said she would like that very much, and they rose and embraced and parted and did not know, then, if that evening would ever come.

Mohsin Hamid is one of the most inventive and empathetic narrators of our time

He writes with a finger on the world's rapid pulse and with keen feeling for its citizens. He portrays people unmoored by change, yet dreaming of their origins. He explores the clashes and commonalities of cultures and the individuals they contain; the pull of ambition and the sway of zealotry and corruption; the tug of migration and what it means to call a place home. A master stylist, he is a pioneer of form, with each new work creating a new way to tell the tale. He's tender and wry, sharply aware of shifting political currents, attuned to intimacies that link us all. He mirrors us back to ourselves, and enlists us— yearning, questing, and, in spite of everything, ardent for connection— in the story.

MOTH SMOKE

A steamy love story, a noir thriller, a portrait of Pakistan in the throes of change

When Daru Shezad is fired from his banking job in Lahore, he begins a decline that plummets the length of this smart and darkly funny tale. Before long, Daru can't pay his bills, loses his toehold among Pakistan's elite, and, as if he wasn't in enough trouble, falls in love with the beautiful and restless wife of a childhood friend and rival. Desperate to reverse his fortunes, he embarks on a career in crime, only to find himself on trial for a murder he may not

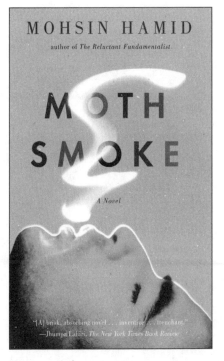

have committed—an uncertainty of fate that mirrors that of his country.

"A first novel of remarkable wit, poise, profundity, and strangeness . . . *Moth Smoke* is a treat." —*Esquire*

"Stunning . . . a hip page turner." —*Los Angeles Times*

HOW TO GET FILTHY RICH IN RISING ASIA

The bestselling and unforgettable tale of a poor boy's quest for wealth and love

In a sprawling metropolis, a nameless hero begins to amass an empire built on that most fluid—and increasingly scarce—of goods: water. Yet our hero's heart is fixated on something else—the pretty girl whose star rises along with his, their paths crossing and recrossing over the years, a lifelong affair sparked and snuffed and sparked again by the forces that careen their fates along. Stealing its shape from the self-help books devoured across the continent, *How to Get Filthy Rich in Rising Asia* creates two unforgettable characters who manage to find fleeting moments of intimacy in the midst of shattering change.

MOHSIN HAMID

How to Get Filthy Rich in Rising Asia

A NOVEL

"Audacious...Hamid reaffirms his place as one of his generation's most inventive and gifted writers." —MICHIKO KAKUTANI, *The New York Times*

"Marvelous and moving."   —*Time*

"Extraordinarily clever . . . Hamid has taken the most American form of literature—the self-help book—and transformed it to tell . . . a surprisingly moving story."   —**Ron Charles, *The Washington Post***

DISCONTENT AND ITS CIVILIZATIONS
DISPATCHES FROM LAHORE, NEW YORK, AND LONDON

A penetrating and deeply personal portrait of our tumultuous times

A "water lily" who has called three countries on three continents his home, Mohsin Hamid writes with truly panoramic perspective about the forces that are transforming contemporary life. Here he traces the fracture lines generated by a decade and a half of seismic change, from the "war on terror" to the struggles of individuals to maintain humanity in the rigid face of ideology or the indifferent face of globalization. In essays that have all the electricity, inventiveness, and sly imagination of his novels, he brings a dazzlingly diverse global culture within emotional and intellectual reach.

"One of his generation's most inventive and gifted writers."
—**Michiko Kakutani,** *The New York Times*

"A master critic of the modern global condition." ——*Foreign Policy*